BIG IDEAS in SCIENCE

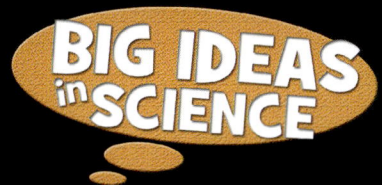

SPLITTING THE ATOM

Katie Parker

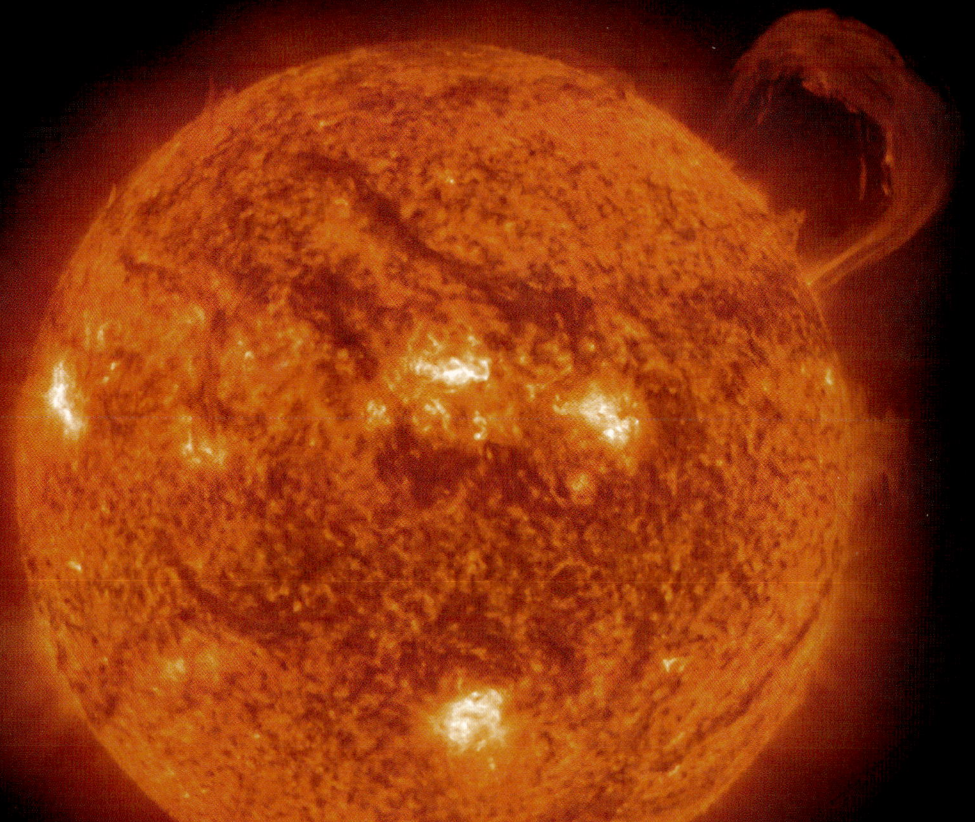

This edition first published in 2010 in the United States of America
by Marshall Cavendish Benchmark.

Marshall Cavendish Benchmark
99 White Plains Road
Tarrytown, NY 10591
www.marshallcavendish.us

Copyright © 2010 by Q2AMedia
All rights reserved. No part of this book may be reproduced
in any form without the written permission of Q2AMedia.

All Internet addresses were available and accurate when this book went to press.

Library of Congress Cataloging-in-Publication Data
Parker, Katie, 1974–
Splitting the atom / by Katie Parker.
p. cm. — (Big ideas in science)
Summary: "Provides comprehensive information on the discovery of the atom
and how it affects our lives today"—Provided by publisher.
Includes bibliographical references and index.
ISBN 978-0-7614-4399-5
1. Atoms—Juvenile literature.
2. Nuclear physics—Juvenile literature. I. Title.
QC173.16.P37 2010
539.7—dc22
2009000126

Cover: NASA, Andrea Danti/Shutterstock
Half Title: NASA.
p4tl: NASA; p4tc: NASA; p4tr: Shutterstock; p5tl: Dreamstime; p5tc: Shutterstock; p5tr: Shutterstock;
p5tr: Shutterstock; p6: Mary Evans Picture Library/Photolibrary; p10: BigStockPhoto; p14: Corbis;
p15: Rich Frishman/Getty Images; p16: moodboard/Corbis; p17bl: Björn Kindler/iStockPhoto;
p17tr: Shutterstock; p18: Bettmann/Corbis; p20: Corbis; p25: iStockphoto; p26: Photolibrary;
p27: Science Faction/Getty Images; p28: Erik Freeland/Corbis; p29: The Stock Asylum, LLC/Alamy;
pp30-31: NASA; p31t: Bettmann/Corbis; p32: El Comandante; p33: Nicolas Delerue; p34: NASA;
p36: NASA; p37: NASA; p38: NASA; p39: CERN; p43: Mary Evans Picture Library/Photolibrary;
p44: Berkeley Lab's Roy Kaltschmidt/U.S. Department of Energy; p45: NASA.
Illustrations: Q2AMedia Art Bank

Created by Q2AMedia
Art Director: Sumit Charles
Editor: Denise Pangia
Series Editor: Penny Dowdy
Client Service Manager: Santosh Vasudevan
Project Manager: Shekhar Kapur
Designer: Shilpi Sarkar
Illustrator: Prachand Kumar
Photo research: Shreya Sharma

Printed in Malaysia

1 3 5 6 4 2

Contents

The Heart of the Matter	4
Discovering the Atom	6
Elements	10
Radiation	14
Energetic Nuclei	18
Nuclear Fission	22
Nuclear Medicine	26
Dropping the Bomb	30
Nuclear Fusion	34
Exploring Space with Atomic Energy	38
The Subatomic Zoo	42
Glossary	46
Find Out More	47
Index	48

solar system

Earth in solar system

city on Earth

The Heart of the Matter

Everything is connected to everything. Do you know how?

You may not think so, but you have something in common with every organism on Earth, from a single-celled bacterium to a great blue whale. You also have something in common with rocks and rivers and air. In fact, everything you can see—and can't see—is connected by one common bond.

You're also connected to things in space. That's right! The brightest star you can see has something in common with you. In fact, everything in the universe is connected to everything else. What is this connection? **Matter**.

All of the objects in the diagram above are examples of matter, or things that take up space. How much matter each object has is called its **mass**. But matter is formed from something that has almost no mass at all. **Particles** of matter make up atoms. These atoms form elements,

From the largest thing to the smallest thing, everything you can see—and can't see—is made of tiny particles called atoms.

which are the building blocks of matter. Elements combine in different ways to form **molecules**. For example, hydrogen and oxygen are both elements. If you combine two hydrogen atoms and one oxygen atom, you get a water molecule—H_2O! Put billions of water molecules together, and you have something to drink!

Everything in the universe is made of matter. You can break down anything—a computer, a strand of hair, a tree—into smaller and smaller pieces until you eventually divide it into atoms. Of course, atoms are much too small for any of us to see. For example, if you lined up seventy million (that's 70,000,000) helium atoms in a row, they would fit across a pencil eraser!

You can break an atom into even smaller pieces, called subatomic particles. These particles, though, will no longer have the qualities of the atom. For example, one atom of gold has all the qualities that make gold shiny and beautiful. If you broke the atoms into pieces, those qualities would no longer exist.

Scientists are very interested in the invisible world of atoms. You are about to find out how amazing the subatomic universe can be.

> The way atoms are arranged is very important in any kind of matter. If atoms are packed tightly together, the matter will be a solid. If they are loose, the matter will be a liquid. If they are far apart, the matter will be a gas. The air you breathe is made of atoms that are far apart.

Discovering the Atom

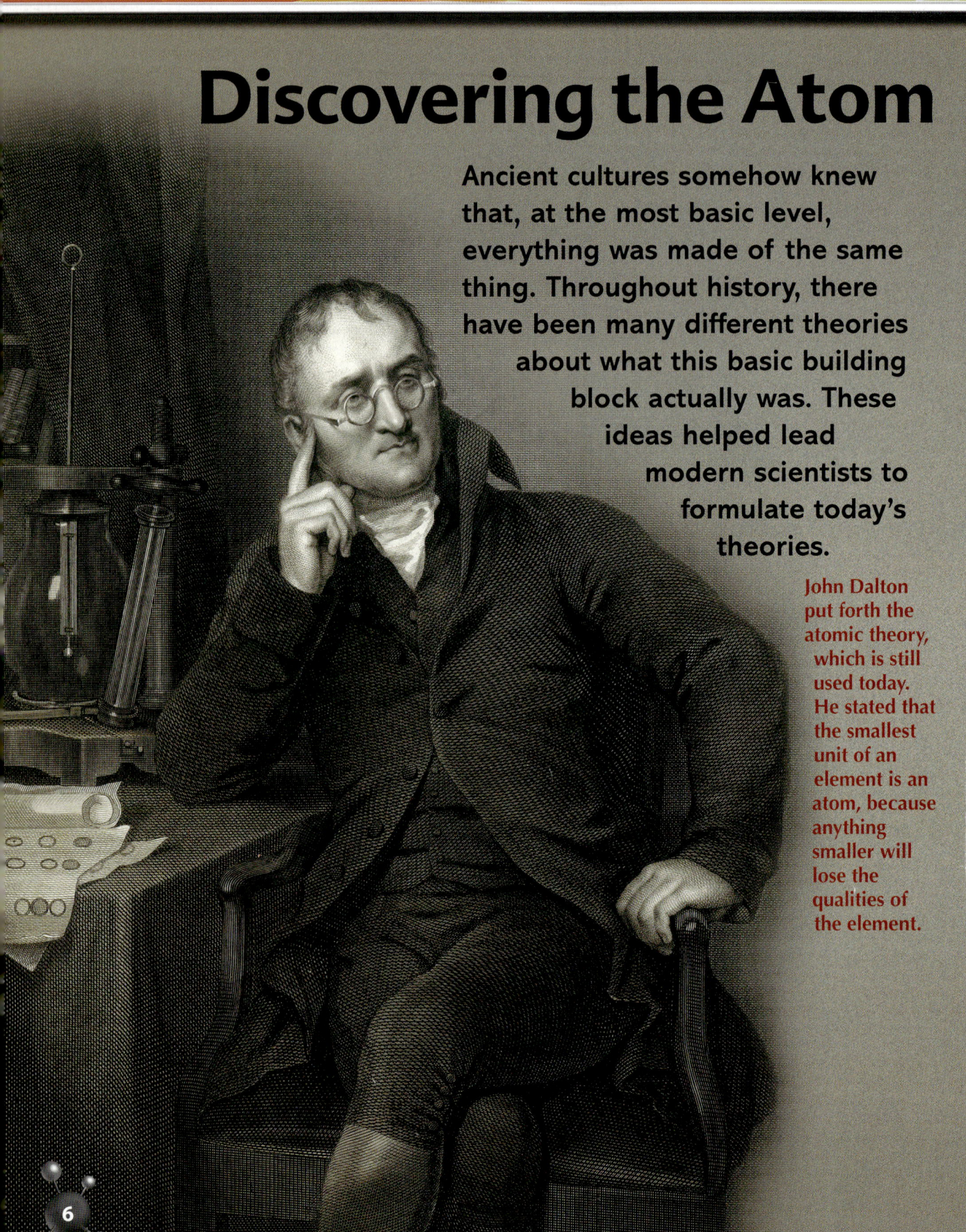

Ancient cultures somehow knew that, at the most basic level, everything was made of the same thing. Throughout history, there have been many different theories about what this basic building block actually was. These ideas helped lead modern scientists to formulate today's theories.

John Dalton put forth the atomic theory, which is still used today. He stated that the smallest unit of an element is an atom, because anything smaller will lose the qualities of the element.

Humans have a long history of searching for answers about our universe. Around 600 B.C.E., an ancient Greek philosopher named Thales was trying to identify the substance that he believed was used to make everything in the world. He concluded that the common bond was water. About two hundred years later, another Greek philosopher named Empedocles challenged Thales's theory. According to Empedocles, it was much more sensible to believe that everything in the world was made of several elements. These elements included earth, air, fire, and water.

Around the same time that Empedocles presented his theory, a philosopher named Democritus started to wonder about water. Water is the only substance on Earth that can be found in nature in all three states: gas, liquid, and solid. How did it change from a gas, to a liquid, to a solid? Even more interesting was this question: How could a solid change into a liquid, and then change back again? Somewhere in the water there must be some small, invisible particle that does not change. That particle, he claimed, was an atom. In Greek, the word *atom* means, "a thing that cannot be divided."

Finally, in 1803, John Dalton came up with a new theory: the atomic theory. He stated that matter was made of atoms. He also stated that atoms were

No one has actually ever seen an atom to this day. No microscope is powerful enough to view one. How small is an atom? Think about the number of leaves on one tree. Now think about the number of leaves on all the trees around the world. It's an unimaginable number! In one single drop of water there are more atoms than leaves on Earth!

the smallest unit of an element, because anything smaller than an atom would lose the qualities of the element.

In 1897 more advances were made by a scientist named J. J. Thomson. Thomson's experiments involved running electricity through different kinds of elements in a specially designed tube. No matter what the element was, it gave off something called a cathode ray, which is made of negatively charged particles.

This led Thomson to hypothesize, or suggest, that atoms themselves were made up of even smaller particles. He called these particles "corpuscles," although we now call them **electrons**. Thomson believed that the electricity was pulling the electrons away from the atoms. This in turn caused the atoms to become positively charged. As a result of these experiments, Thomson concluded that the atom was a positively charged ball, with negative charges floating inside the ball. Today, his model of the atom is called the plum pudding model.

Positively charged matter

Electrons

In the plum pudding model, an atom is a positively charged ball with negatively charged particles floating inside.

7

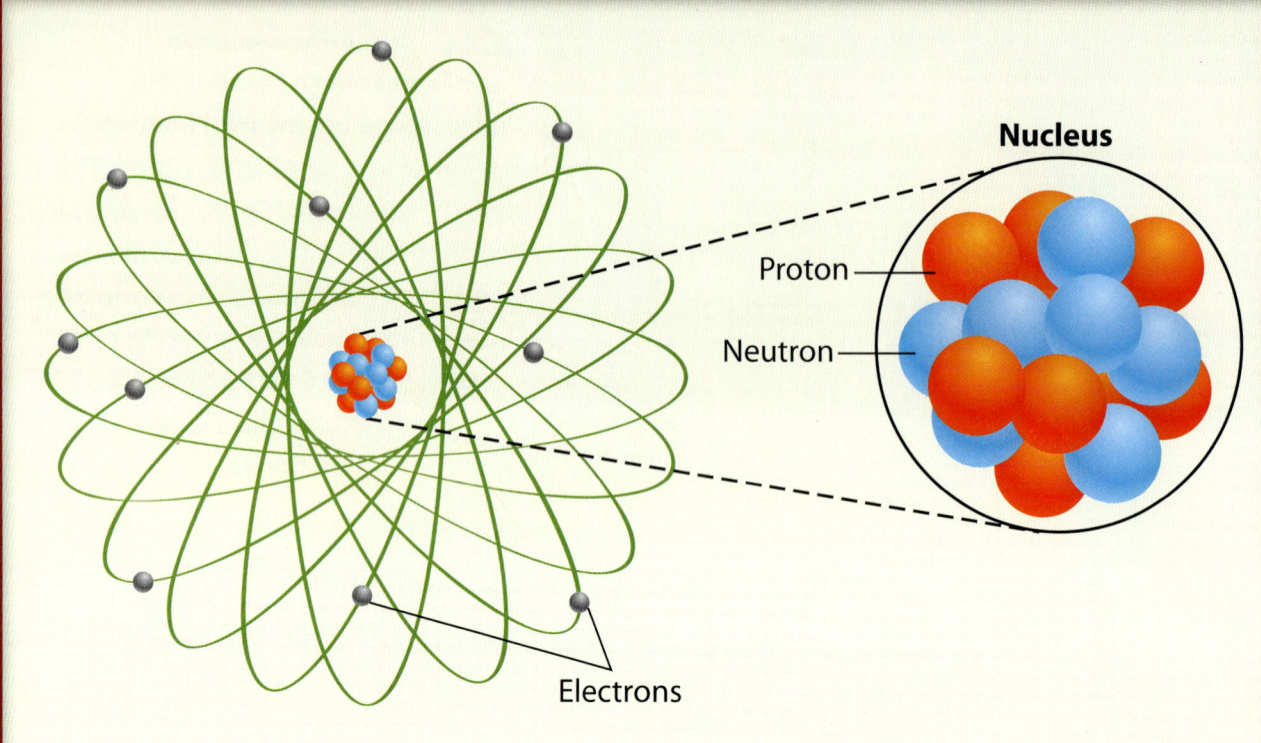

The Rutherford atomic model has been proven to be the most accurate model. It shows that protons and neutrons are found inside a nucleus, and that electrons orbit around that nucleus.

Scientists continued exploring the atom. Perhaps by understanding the smallest part of matter, they could understand the larger picture. They knew that the atom had negative and positive electrical charges. Scientists also knew that the positive and negative charges were attracted to each other. Could this be all that was holding atoms together?

In 1911 a scientist named Ernest Rutherford conducted an experiment to test the plum pudding atomic model. He bombarded, or repeatedly hit, gold foil with fast-moving positive charges, called alpha particles. He noticed that most of the positive particles passed right through the foil, as he expected. Some, though, were wildly deflected, or pushed off course. A few even bounced directly back. It was as if the particles were repelled, or forced away, by the atom. According to the plum pudding model, this shouldn't happen. The negative electrons should attract the positive charges.

Rutherford conducted more experiments. He figured out that an atom must have a heavy nucleus, or center, that is made of **protons**, or positively charged particles. The nucleus also contains **neutrons**, which have no charge at all. So although negatively charged electrons were orbiting the nucleus, the heavier nucleus had a stronger positive charge. This is why some particles were deflected.

Rutherford discovered the nucleus and created the atomic model that we still use today. Now that we know what the actual building blocks of matter are, let's return to water. What exactly is water? It is a substance made of two different elements: hydrogen and oxygen. Two hydrogen atoms share electrons with one oxygen atom. Together, these atoms form a single water molecule.

When an atom forms a molecule, energy is released. Scientists in the early twentieth century were very interested in learning the source of this energy. Who knew what could be done with the power that these tiny mysteries possessed?

> Water is a clear, tasteless, odorless substance. In fact, it's probably the most unique substance on Earth. It is the only substance that can be found in nature in all three forms: liquid, solid, and gas. Water's unique properties are one of the reasons life on Earth is possible.

All molecules are made of atoms that have joined together. When a water molecule forms, two hydrogen atoms bond to an oxygen atom.

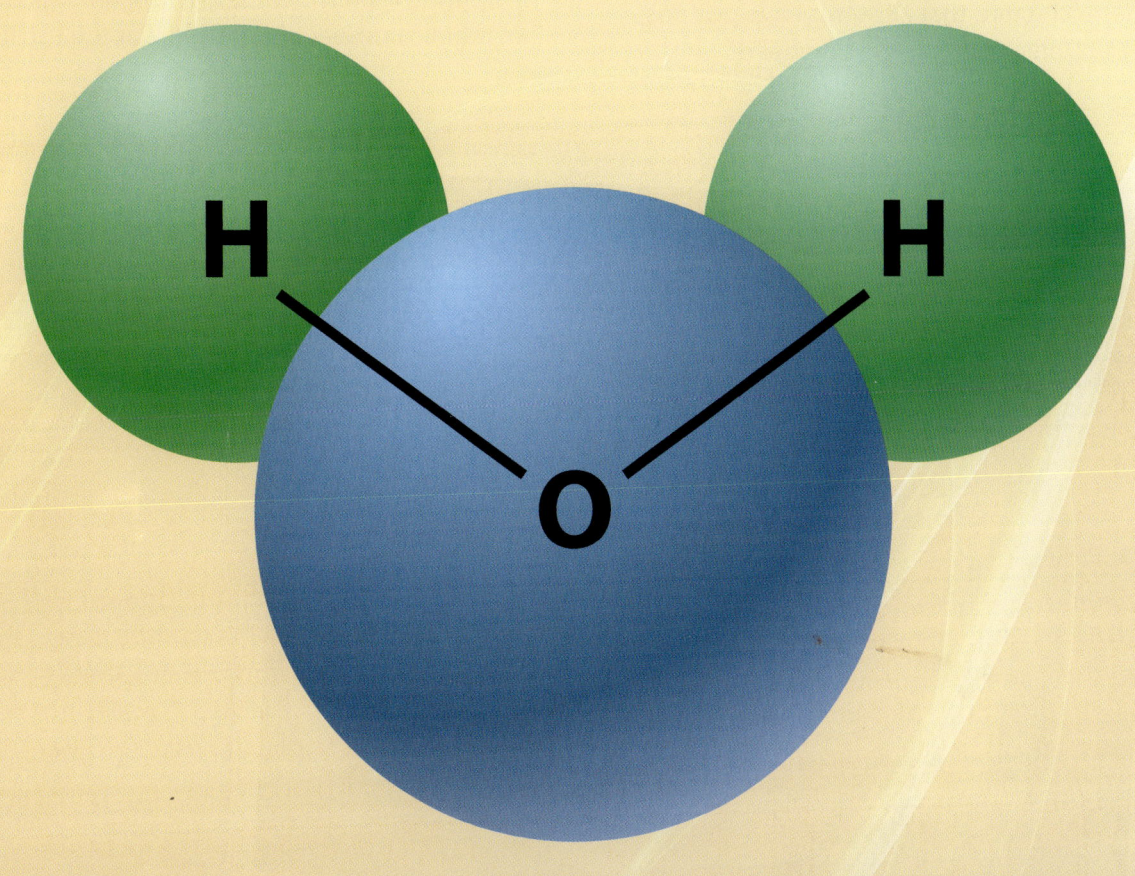

Elements

It can be hard to understand the difference between atoms and elements. Yet, it's a very important difference. As scientists have learned, some elements are much more common than others.

Atoms are the building blocks of elements. One atom of the element gold is a tiny amount, but if you put enough gold atoms together, you will have a larger piece of gold. However, if you have one atom of gold and you remove even one proton or electron, you have changed the atom and it is no longer the element gold.

Each element has different properties. Rutherford stated that all atoms have protons and electrons. However, the number of subatomic particles varies. The number of protons in an atom determines what element it is. For example, carbon has six protons. Hydrogen has one proton and is the least massive element. Uranium has ninety-two protons and is the most massive element found in nature. The number of protons in the nucleus of an atom is its **atomic number**. The periodic table of elements lists all the elements that have been discovered so far. The elements are listed on the table in order of increasing atomic number. Hydrogen, which has an atomic number of 1, is always at the top left.

Gold is a metallic element.

The periodic table of elements is organized by atomic number, or the number of protons in the nucleus of one atom of each element.

The periodic table is also organized so that elements in the same vertical column have similar properties. They are given group or family names such as metals and nonmetals.

Some elements are used in their pure form. Hydrogen is used in rocket fuel. Nitrogen is used in fertilizer. Mercury is used in batteries. Others are more commonly found in combination. You have just learned that a molecule of water is formed when atoms of the element hydrogen combine with an atom of the element oxygen. Carbon dioxide is a molecule, too. It is made from one carbon atom and two oxygen atoms.

Scientists can now make elements. Technitium was the first element ever made. It has several uses now. Doctors inject it during medical procedures. It emits particles as it moves through the body. Doctors can follow the path of the particles to locate tumors and to see damage caused by a heart attack, among other things inside the body.

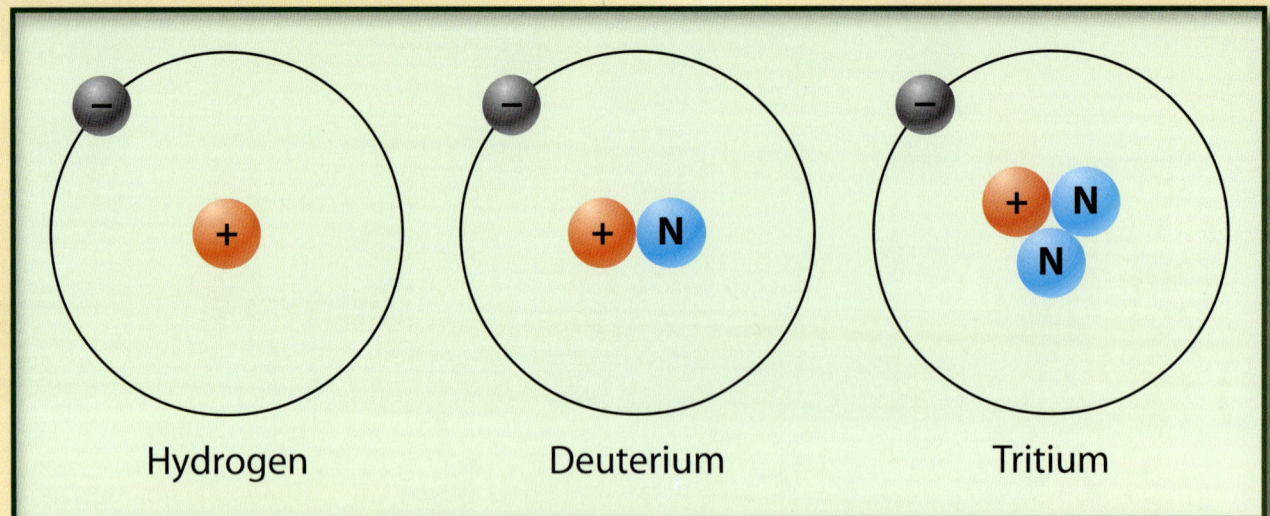

Isotopes of an element have the same number of protons, but the number of neutrons may change. These are all isotopes of the element hydrogen.

To learn more about elements, scientists studied stable atoms, which are atoms that are not likely to change into other atoms or release energy. Yet, they learned even more by looking at unstable atoms, which are more likely to release energy by changing into another atom.

Ions, or charged atoms, are unstable. They form when an electron leaves an atom's orbit, or a new one enters it. When an electron leaves, the atom has more protons than electrons. It has a positive charge. When a new electron joins an atom, the atom has more electrons than protons. Now it has a negative charge. Ions are more likely to form molecules than stable atoms are. When a molecule is formed, energy is released.

Isotopes are atoms of an element with the same number of protons, but a different number of neutrons in their nucleus. This means that an isotope has a different atomic mass. Many of these

All organisms have carbon-14, which is an unstable isotope of carbon, in their cells. When the cells die, carbon-14 decays at a steady rate. Since carbon-14 is radioactive, it has something called a half-life, which is the time it takes for half of the carbon-14 atoms to decay. Archaeologists can measure the amount of carbon-14 left in an organism, which helps determine the organism's age. This is known as carbon-14 dating. It can be used to estimate the age of organic remains up to 50,000 years old. Giant mammals from the Ice Age can be dated using carbon-14. However, after 50,000 years, all the carbon-14 will have decayed and there will be nothing for scientists to measure.

isotopes are unstable. Unstable isotopes are **radioactive**. Remember that the number of protons in the nucleus is an atom's atomic number. The number of protons and neutrons is its atomic mass. Compared to the nucleus, electrons do not add much mass to an atom.

For example, uranium is an element. All forms of uranium atoms must have ninety-two protons. Uranium-238 is the most common form of uranium. It is named for its atomic mass. Atoms of uranium-238 have 146 neutrons in their nuclei.

Uranium-235 has 143 neutrons in the nucleus. Both are uranium isotopes. They have the same atomic number: 92.

Carbon-14 is an isotope of carbon-12. Like all isotopes, it undergoes a process called radioactive decay, which is when an isotope spontaneously changes into another atom as it ages. Why does this happen? The atom is unstable. It becomes more stable by decaying. An isotope can take thousands of years to decay.

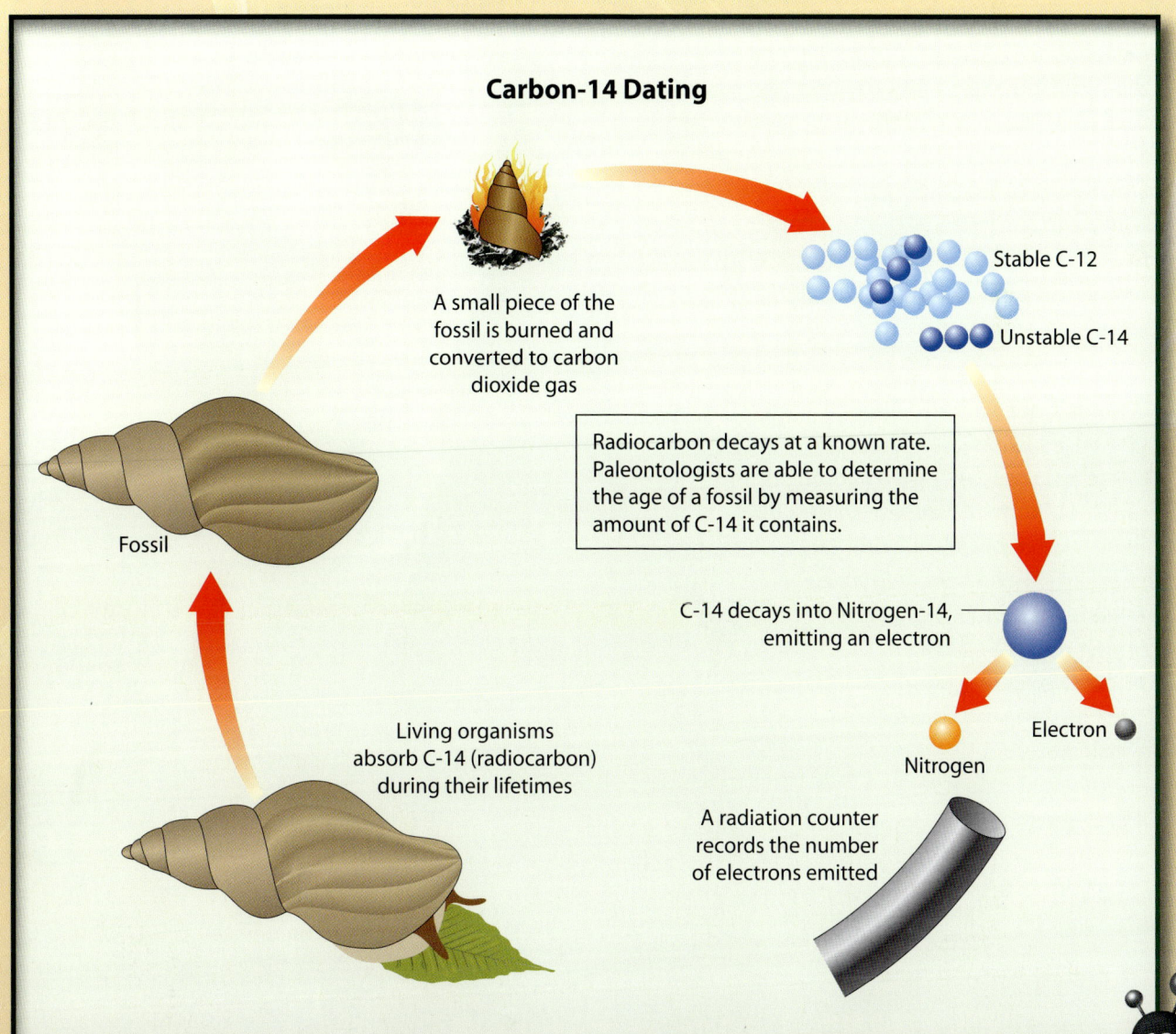

Carbon-14 Dating

A small piece of the fossil is burned and converted to carbon dioxide gas

Stable C-12
Unstable C-14

Fossil

Radiocarbon decays at a known rate. Paleontologists are able to determine the age of a fossil by measuring the amount of C-14 it contains.

C-14 decays into Nitrogen-14, emitting an electron

Electron
Nitrogen

Living organisms absorb C-14 (radiocarbon) during their lifetimes

A radiation counter records the number of electrons emitted

13

Radiation

As an isotope decays, it releases energy known as radiation. Scientists thought this was worth looking into.

In 1896 a French physicist named Antoine Henri Becquerel was working with the element uranium. He wanted to understand why it glowed. He decided to try exposing it to bright sunlight after it had been left in the dark. To prepare, he wrapped the sample of uranium in black paper and left it on a clear photographic plate. He was surprised to find that the uranium left a black print. He assumed the glow caused the plate to turn black. He tried other experiments to prove his assumption. He even placed the uranium in a drawer. Still, an impression appeared. He concluded that it was invisible energy, not light, turning the photographic plate black. Becquerel had discovered radioactivity.

Marie Curie was also experimenting with such substances. Curie knew that light and energy moved by a process called **radiation**. She coined the term *radioactive* to describe elements that constantly emitted energy in this way. She was able to measure the amount of energy coming out of a sample of the radioactive metal radium. There was enough energy to heat water 36.1 degrees Fahrenheit (2.3 degrees Celsius) each hour.

Marie Curie was an important figure in the research of radioactive materials.

It may not sound like a lot of energy, but it was a big discovery. The heated water proved that energy was radiating from, or given off by, the radium. But how was the energy being created?

Today, scientists have that answer. An atom has energy stored in its nucleus. Some elements and isotopes are unstable. They try to become stable by radiating energy that is in the nucleus. As an element decays, it emits particles, which can be either charged or neutral. As this happens, the atom may change into a different element.

Now that the source of this energy is known, it can be measured. A tool called a Geiger counter can measure radiation coming from an element. Radioactive elements can occur naturally. These elements can also be made artificially when scientists add or remove particles from the nucleus of an atom.

In 1958 the United States launched *Explorer 1*. As *Explorer* orbited Earth, a Geiger counter on board began ticking. Scientists realized that this meant a radioactive band encircled Earth! The band was named the Van Allen radiation belt. It is held in place by Earth's magnetic field. Even though the belt is radioactive, it does not pose a threat to life on Earth. In fact, it serves as a buffer against solar winds and radiation!

Geiger counters can measure radiation from space, and any that occurs on Earth. Not all radiation is natural—some is made by people.

Why do we create radioactive materials? We do it because scientists have found many uses for radiation. For example, because of carbon-14 dating, we have a better idea of the history of life on Earth. Yet, carbon-14 has its limits. It can only date decomposing remains, not rocks. Also, it cannot date anything older than 50,000 years. Compared to the age of our Earth, this is a short period of time.

Suppose a fossil is found in a layer of rocks. Uranium-235 can be used to date the rocks and fossils that are much older than 50,000 years. Scientists can also use uranium-235 to date the rocks above and below the fossil. They will know that the fossil's age is somewhere in between.

Radiation has many uses in the medical community.

> Radioactive decay can be compared to making popcorn! Uranium-235 turns into a form of lead when it decays. It cannot be changed back. When you heat corn kernels, they change into popcorn. They cannot be changed back, either.

Radiation also has many uses in the medical community. X rays involve radiation passing through your body and developing into a picture. X rays help doctors find broken bones and other problems within the body. Radiation can also be used to treat cancer. Cancer occurs when a group of cells grows uncontrollably or invades nearby tissue. Over time, a mass of tissue, called a tumor, forms. Radiation can be used to destroy those tumors. It can also be aimed directly at the tumor to minimize the damage to surrounding healthy tissue.

Radiation can be as dangerous as it is helpful. It can harm normal, healthy cells the same way it kills cancer cells. Radioactive atoms can actually change atoms within the body. They can steal electrons or neutrons from the nucleus of a cell's atom.

Radioactive gases are very dangerous. They are marked with brightly colored signs and special warning symbols.

Radioactive atoms can even cause mutations, or mistakes, in a cell's **DNA**. The mutations are reproduced each time the cell divides. If a person is overexposed to radiation, he or she can suffer burns, rashes, and hair loss. Radiation can even cause organ failure, which can be fatal.

Although there are many dangers of radioactivity, there are also many uses for it. How else can it be useful? Here's a clue: radioactivity is energy.

17

Energetic Nuclei

Until the twentieth century, scientists believed that the atom could not be split. John Dalton even stated this in his atomic theory. Yet, radiation from isotopes indicated there must be energy in an atom. Scientists wanted to harness that energy and began wondering if an atom could be split after all.

Then, in 1905, Albert Einstein proposed something radical. He stated that mass and energy were forms of the same thing. You may have heard of his famous equation: $E = mc^2$. The relationship between energy and matter is what this equation is all about!

First, understand that Einstein's Special Theory of Relativity is based on atoms moving at very high speeds. They move almost as fast as the speed of light. Light travels at 186,000 miles (300,000 kilometers) per second. Nothing else travels that fast. Why?

Because of Einstein's Special Theory of Relativity, scientists realized that there was energy inside the nucleus of an atom—and lots of it.

During World War II, Hungarian physicist Leo Szilard knew Nazi Germany was attempting to build a nuclear weapon based on Einstein's formula. Such a bomb would have enough power to destroy an entire city. Szilard wrote a letter and convinced Einstein to sign it and send it to President Franklin Roosevelt. The letter warned of the Nazis' work and encouraged the United States to develop a similar program. The result was the Manhattan Project, which led to the creation of the atom bomb.

$E = mc^2$

According to Einstein, an object, like an atom, would need a lot of energy to travel at such speeds. The faster it went, the more energy it would need. The extra energy would actually add mass to the atom.

In other words, energy can turn into mass. So, mass must be able to turn into energy, as well. This also means that the more mass an object has, the more energy it has. Remember $E = mc^2$? In this equation, E stands for energy, m stands for the mass of an object at rest, and c^2 stands for the speed of light squared, or multiplied by itself. Einstein proposed that if you knew the mass of an object, you could find how much energy it has, simply by using his formula.

What does this have to do with atoms? Recall that the nuclei of atoms are more massive than the electrons. When an atom begins to speed up, it gains mass in its nucleus. So, the nucleus of an atom moving at super high speed holds a lot of energy. Scientists wanted to find out just how much!

According to Einstein's Special Theory of Relativity, a high-speed atom would release enormous amounts of energy when its nucleus was split. But could atoms be sped up and split?

19

In 1934 Enrico Fermi was attempting to make radioactive isotopes. He was very successful in bombarding elements with neutrons! He called upon physicist Lise Meitner to help. She brought in Otto Hahn and Fritz Strassmann, also physicists.

The scientists began working with uranium. They found that it had more than one isotope. Uranium is the heaviest natural element. In addition to 92 protons, the nucleus of a uranium atom can hold between 141 and 146 neutrons. In 1938, while looking at a uranium sample they had bombarded with neutrons, the scientists noticed traces of barium. They had turned one element into another! Hahn realized that the nuclei of some uranium atoms had burst because of all the energy, creating nuclei of a different atomic number and mass. They had produced barium by splitting the atom!

Lise Meitner never received credit for her work on atomic energy.

The scientists published their findings. They had actually split the nucleus of an atom. They called the process **nuclear fission**.

A physicist named Niels Bohr drew a model to show how nuclear fission was possible. His model of the nucleus is called the liquid drop model. Bohr theorized that an atom's nucleus could be compared to a raindrop. It keeps its shape due to surface forces. The energy from the impact of a neutron distorts the nucleus, causing it to change shape. When this happens, the nucleus will be stretched and weakened. It will then split into two atoms that are about the same size. As the nucleus splits, it releases the energy that was once holding the subatomic particles together. The original nucleus splits into two new nuclei with different atomic numbers and masses. They are two different elements!

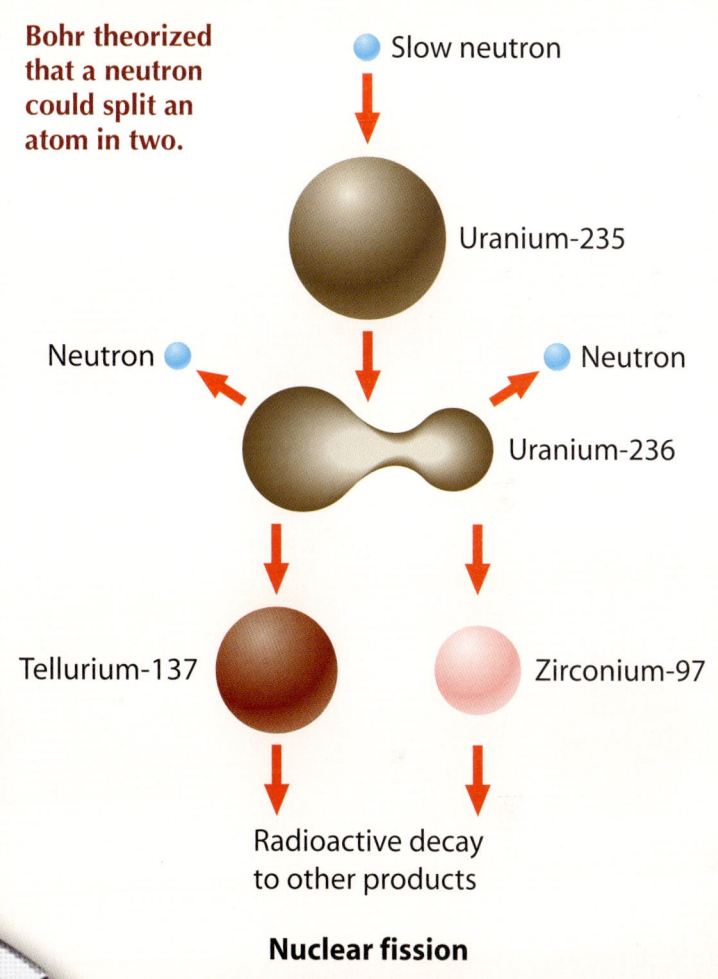

Bohr theorized that a neutron could split an atom in two.

Nuclear fission

Lise Meitner was a great physicist. Yet, she received very little recognition for her work. She was a Jewish woman living in Austria in the late 1930s. It was a dangerous place and time for jews. When the Nazis took over in 1938, she fled the country. Still, Hahn and Strassmann kept her involved in their experiments and discoveries. Hahn won a Nobel Prize for this work in 1945. Meitner went unrecognized. The institute that awards the Nobel Prize has never corrected this mistake. She is the only woman, however, who has an element named after her: meitnerium.

Finally, scientists had found their answers. They knew that an atom could be split. They also knew that nuclear fission released energy. Now they began searching for ways to put that energy to good use.

21

Nuclear Fission

Nuclear fission reactions can create a lot of energy. How can we harness this energy in order to use it?

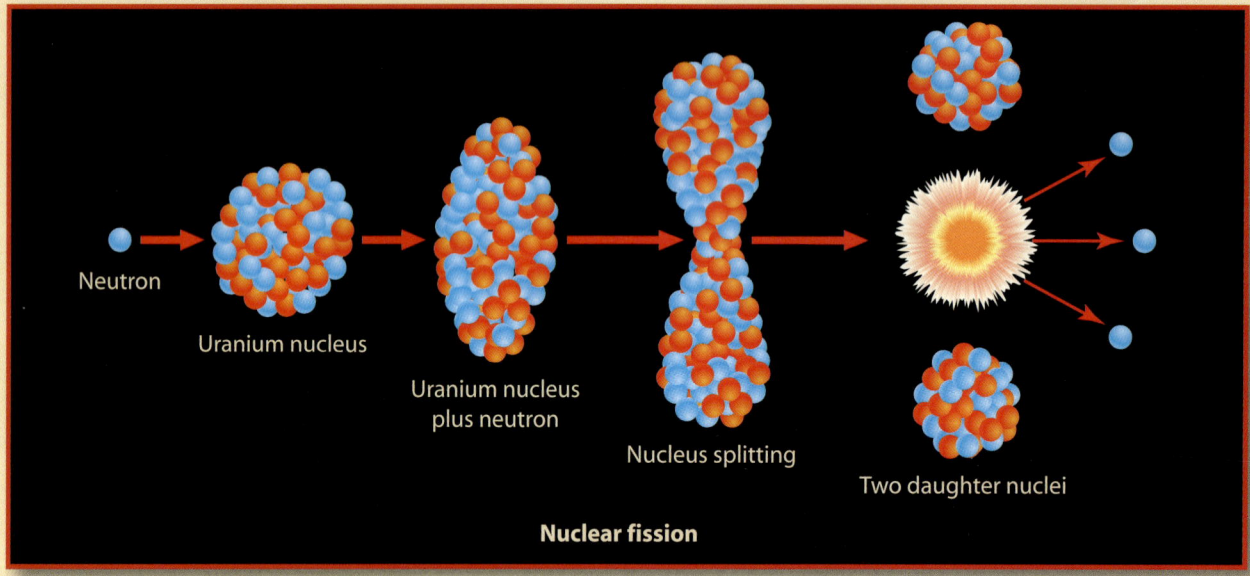

Nuclear fission

The diagram above shows a nuclear fission reaction in detail. A neutron strikes and enters a uranium atom's nucleus. The nucleus splits into two daughter nuclei. The new atoms are lighter elements. Three neutrons are also released. These newly freed neutrons can cause fission reactions in other atoms, which will in turn release their own neutrons. If all the fission reactions take place in a contained area, the energy can be harnessed. That's just what happens in a nuclear power plant.

Uranium-235 is an isotope that occurs naturally. It also decays naturally. As it does so, it emits radiation. So, uranium-235 is a fissile isotope, which means it is capable of undergoing a chain reaction of nuclear fission. If bombarded with neutrons, its nucleus will become unstable and split. Uranium-235 is commonly used to generate nuclear energy, which is the energy that comes from fission reactions.

At a nuclear power plant, enough neutrons from a fission reaction cause more reactions to sustain a chain reaction. Enormous amounts of energy and heat are produced with each reaction.

When nuclear fission occurs, energy is released along with neutrons that strike other uranium nuclei, creating more fission reactions. In a power plant, this continues as a chain reaction. The more reactions occur, the more nuclei and neutrons are made. They become hot and crowded and move even faster. Fission reactions begin to happen faster as a result.

Look at the diagram of the nuclear power plant below. The containment structure keeps any radioactive particles from escaping. Nuclear fission reactions occur in the reactor. Soon it becomes hot and crowded with neutrons and nuclei. This causes the particles to move faster and bump into one another more often. More reactions take place. Control rods are lowered into the reactor to absorb neutrons. This causes the reactions to slow down and allows the reactor to cool. The control rods can be lifted out of the reactor to speed up reactions, too.

The reactor also contains water, which is turned into steam by the heat of the fission reactions. The steam is pumped up and carried to a **turbine**, which causes a **generator** to spin. The nuclear energy is turned into usable electricity.

Almost all uranium found naturally is uranium-238. It cannot sustain a chain of fission reactions, so it cannot be used to produce nuclear energy. However, inside nuclear reactors, uranium is used to trap extra neutrons. It decays into plutonium-239, which is even more fissile than uranium-235. Plutonium-239 releases more neutrons when struck. It is hard to get pure plutonium-239 from uranium-238. Often, it gains an extra neutron (making it plutonium-240). Plutonium-240 is too radioactive to be easily used, so plutonium-239 is the preferred isotope for nuclear fission. Yet, it also heats up much faster, making it riskier to work with.

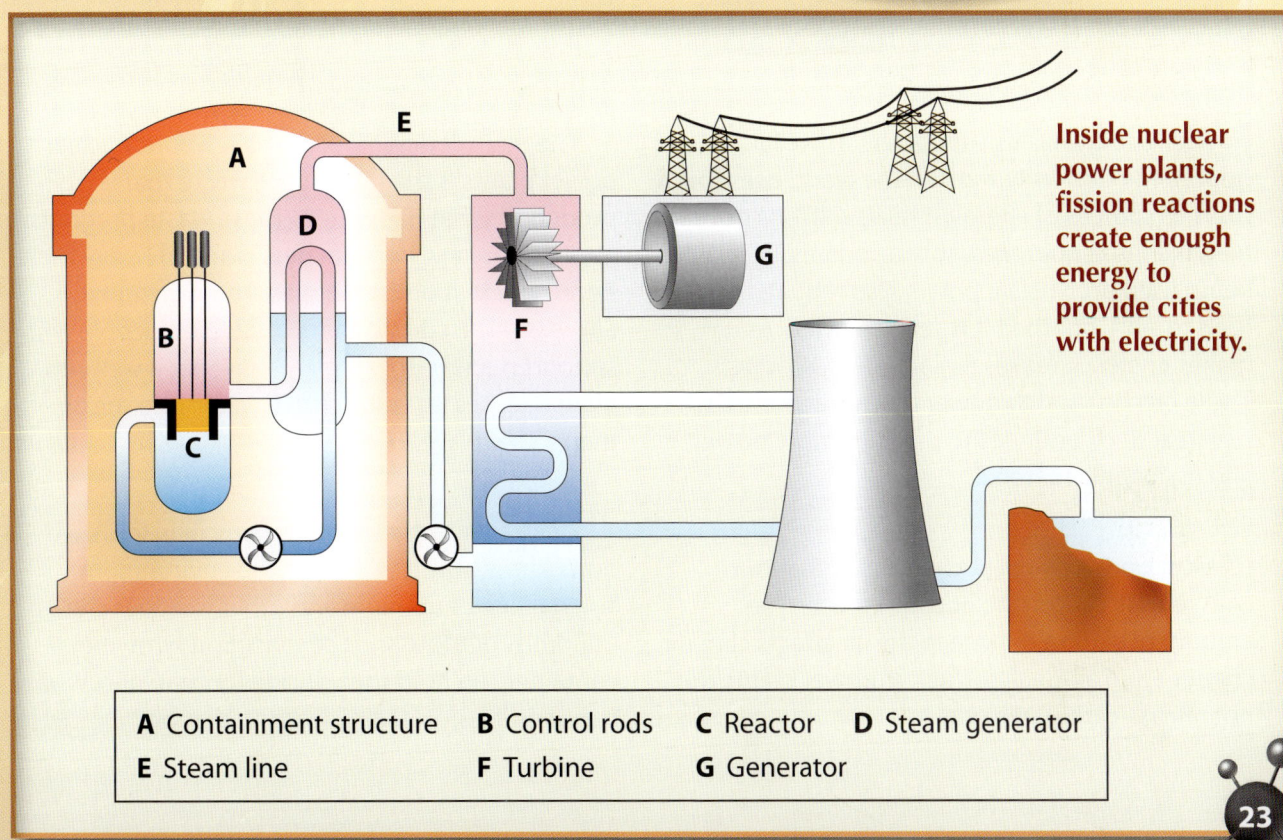

Inside nuclear power plants, fission reactions create enough energy to provide cities with electricity.

A Containment structure	**B** Control rods	**C** Reactor	**D** Steam generator
E Steam line	**F** Turbine	**G** Generator	

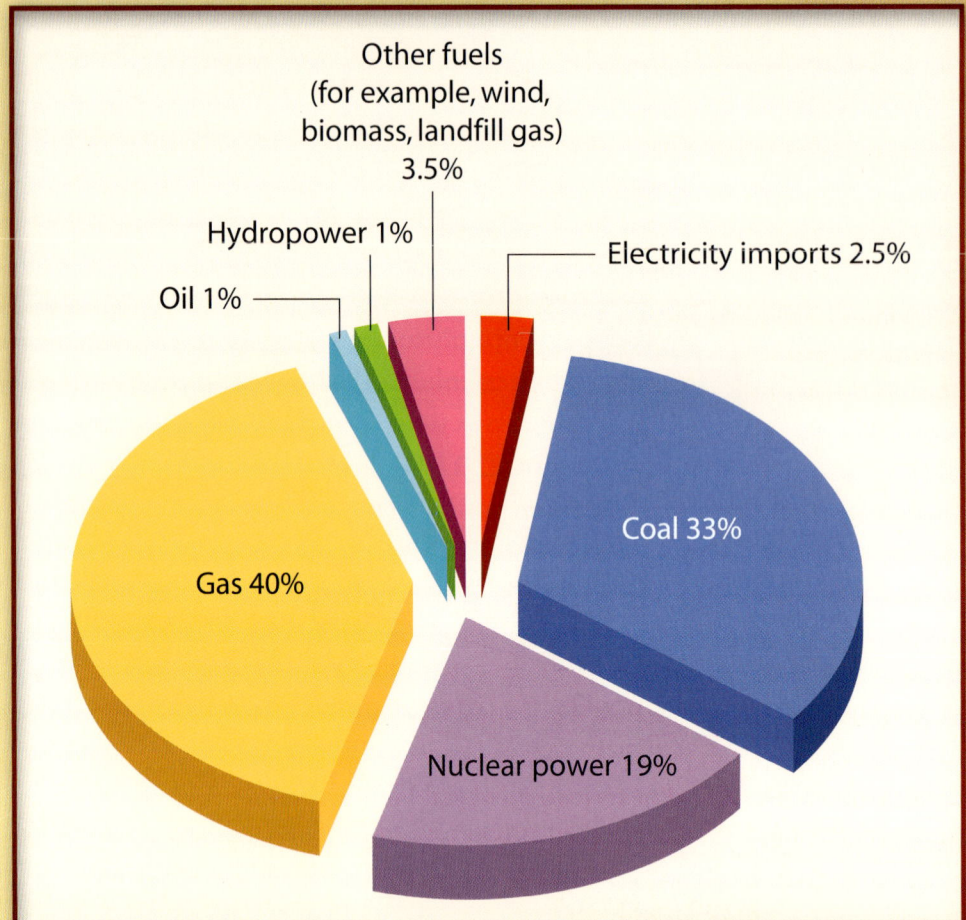

This chart shows what sources the United States used for energy in 2004.

Nuclear energy has its supporters, as well as its opponents. Currently, most of the world uses **fossil fuels** as sources of energy. It takes millions of years to make these nonrenewable resources. They are being used up. Nuclear power also requires fossil fuels to start, but then it is self-renewing. As it makes energy, it makes fissionable byproducts. These can be used to power more reactions. Each new reaction continues to produce more power and fissionable material.

Most power plants, such as those that burn coal, release carbon dioxide into the air. The amount of carbon dioxide in the air affects climate changes and air quality. Nuclear power plants do not release carbon dioxide.

The main concern people have about nuclear power plants is the radioactive waste that is produced. What happens to these waste products? Most of it is kept in containers made of heavy metal, because radiation cannot pass through metal. Some is released into the air. However, people who support nuclear power plants say that a well-run plant releases less radioactive waste into the air than a coal plant.

Since, radioactive waste is fairly new to us, we don't know how it will affect the environment. The half-life of uranium and other isotopes can be hundreds of thousands of years. Surely, no metal container can hold them inside for that long. What happens if a slow leak releases radiation?

We do know what happens during a nuclear leak. In 1986 a nuclear power plant in Chernobyl, Russia, overheated. Radiation was released. People who were exposed suffered severe health problems. Many died because of this disaster.

Tragedies like the one at Chernobyl give nuclear energy a bad name. Yet, in many ways, nuclear energy is much needed.

Most fossil fuels come from mines. Mining ruins landscapes and habitats. It also harms people who live in neighboring communities. Traditional energy plants immediately use the coal they mine, so they continually need more. Nuclear power plants, however, use uranium for approximately three years before they need a new sample.

It is hard to estimate the number of deaths from the Chernobyl fallout, because many people died years later of diseases such as cancer. These cannot be definitely attributed to the accident. Yet, birth defects can be linked to the fallout. Many of the apparently healthy survivors went on to have children with birth defects. The radiation mutated, or changed, the parent's DNA, which was passed on to the baby. Some of these defects may have occurred because many people continued living near the plant, even though the soil and water were heavily contaminated.

Nuclear Medicine

When people hear about nuclear energy, they usually think about its dangers. Yet, splitting the atom has saved a number of lives.

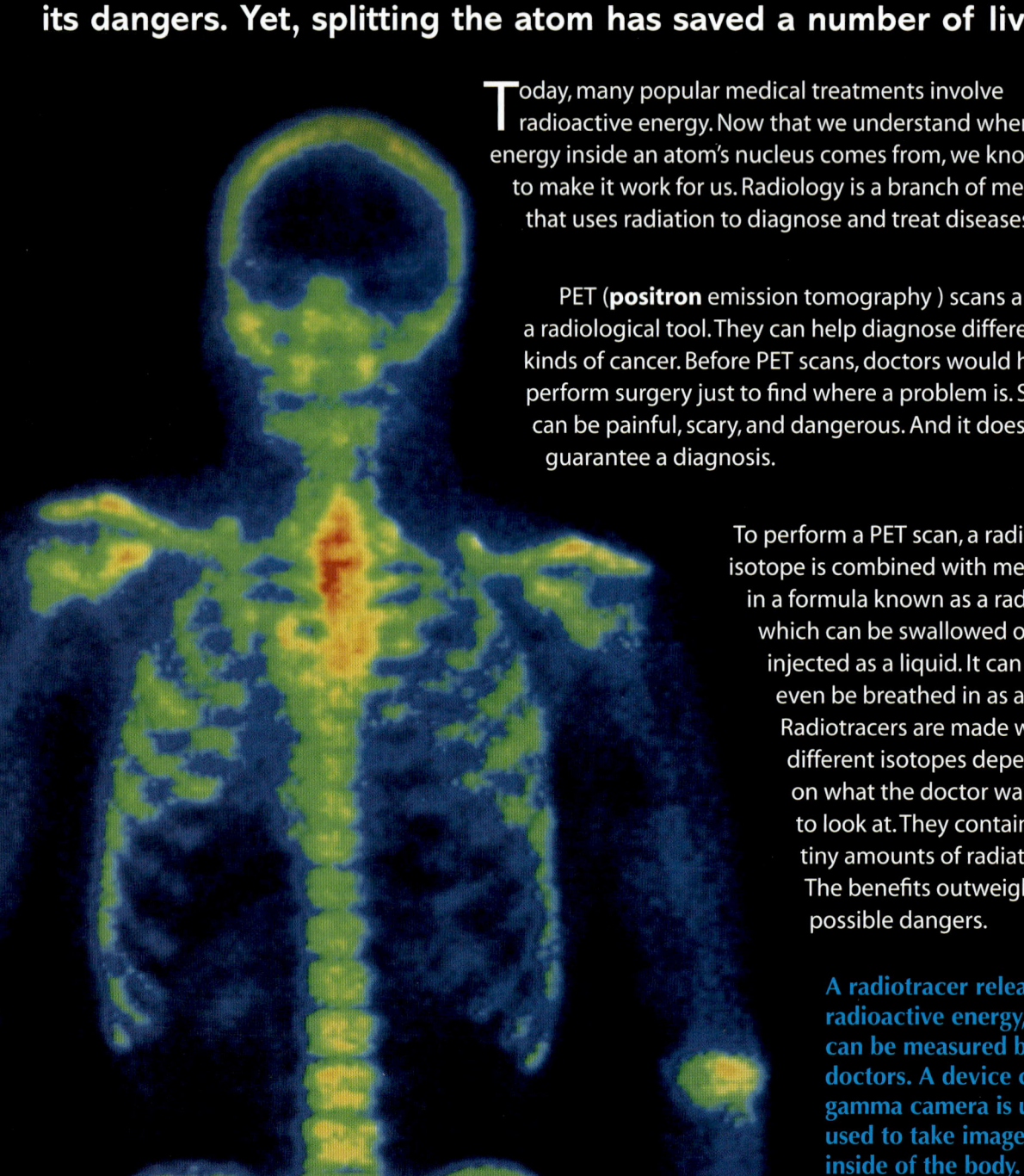

Today, many popular medical treatments involve radioactive energy. Now that we understand where the energy inside an atom's nucleus comes from, we know how to make it work for us. Radiology is a branch of medicine that uses radiation to diagnose and treat diseases.

PET (**positron** emission tomography) scans are a radiological tool. They can help diagnose different kinds of cancer. Before PET scans, doctors would have to perform surgery just to find where a problem is. Surgery can be painful, scary, and dangerous. And it does not guarantee a diagnosis.

To perform a PET scan, a radioactive isotope is combined with medicine in a formula known as a radiotracer, which can be swallowed or injected as a liquid. It can even be breathed in as a gas. Radiotracers are made with different isotopes depending on what the doctor wants to look at. They contain only tiny amounts of radiation. The benefits outweigh the possible dangers.

A radiotracer releases radioactive energy, which can be measured by doctors. A device called a gamma camera is usually used to take images of the inside of the body. This allows doctors to see areas where the radiotracer is more concentrated.

The radiotracer moves through the body. It is absorbed by the organ the doctors want to study. It begins radiating energy in rays. The patient lies in two different machines (a CT, or computed tomography, scanner and PET scanner). These machines measure the amount of energy in the rays. The rays are converted into light. Finally, the light is changed into an image that the doctors can use. Tumors are clearly visible.

A thallium stress test is another diagnostic tool. A patient exercises until the heart rate speeds up. Then, thallium, a radioactive element, is injected into the patient's blood. He or she lies down for a few hours. During that time, thallium moves around the heart. Areas that are not receiving as much blood as they should will not receive the thallium. They will show up dark on the pictures. This indicates that there is not enough blood flowing to the heart.

Wilhelm Conrad Roentgen never graduated high school. Yet, he was smart and he liked to perform experiments. He was also interested in photography. In 1895 he experimented with different ways to develop pictures. During one experiment, he accidentally discovered X rays! He took a picture of his wife's hand, but the image he developed showed her finger bones! His findings were published internationally, along with the picture of his wife's hand. In the article he called the rays "X rays" because he did not know their source. The name stuck.

A thallium stress test is another radiological tool. It tells doctors how well the heart is working. Areas of the heart will appear dark if blood isn't flowing well.

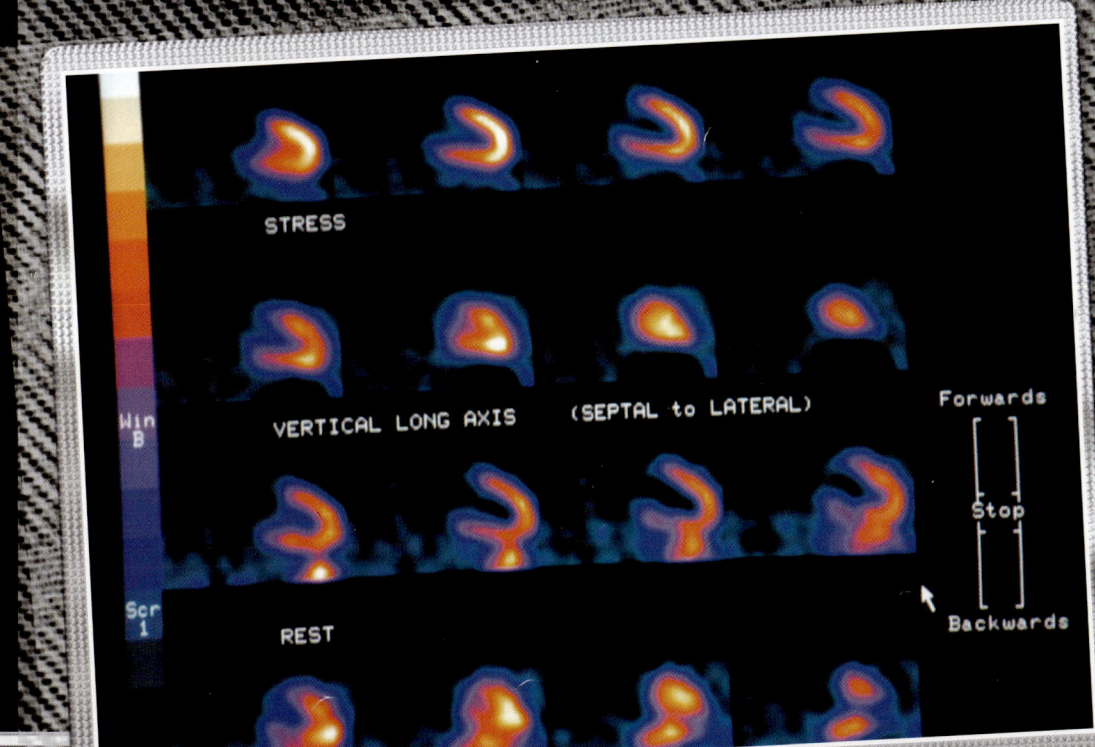

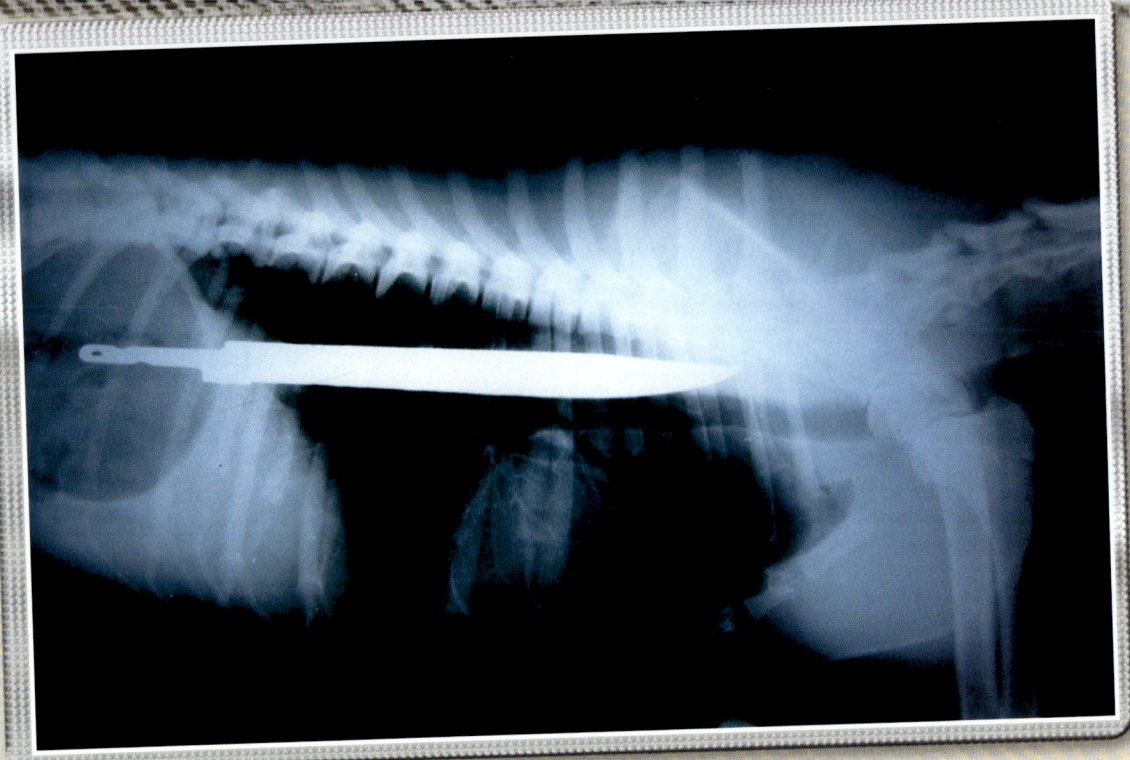

Yikes! This dog jumped up on the table to steal some food and swallowed a knife instead. With the use of X rays, doctors can see the exact position of the knife so they can safely remove it.

X rays are probably the most well-known radiological tool. They take clear pictures of bones. Doctors can use them to tell exactly where a bone has broken. They can also be used to find objects that have been swallowed or have otherwise entered the body.

X rays were first used in 1895. Patients had to travel to have an X ray taken. In 1919 the first portable X-ray machine was invented. Chemist Marie Curie realized how important this machine could be. She used her own money to buy several X-ray machines. She had them placed inside ambulances during World War I. The ambulance staff rescued wounded soldiers and could use the X-ray machine to find bullets.

Most inventors are happy with one invention, but not American inventor Frederick M. Jones. He invented the portable X-ray machine. He also invented the machine that made movies with sound possible. Without him we might still be watching silent movies. He also invented the refrigerated trucks that we use to transport food and medicine. In total, Jones had over sixty inventions in his name!

28

Today, X rays have many other uses. Have you ever been to an airport? Security screeners use X rays to check inside bags. X rays can even find bombs or other explosive devices.

As you learned earlier, radiation is also used to treat cancer. Most cancerous tumors will shrink or disappear during radiation therapy. Patients are placed inside a machine that emits a beam of radiation. The beam is focused on the cancerous area. A linear accelerator is a type of particle accelerator machine that is widely used in medicine. Particle accelerators speed up charged particles.

Linear accelerators enable radiologists to aim the charged particles directly at the cancerous area. The cancerous area is hit with a stronger dose of radiation. Unfortunately, doctors cannot totally spare healthy cells from the radiation. The skin near the treatment area often suffers burns, too.

Particle accelerators have been of recent interest to many scientists. Their applications are just being discovered. Could they help us answer questions about the universe?

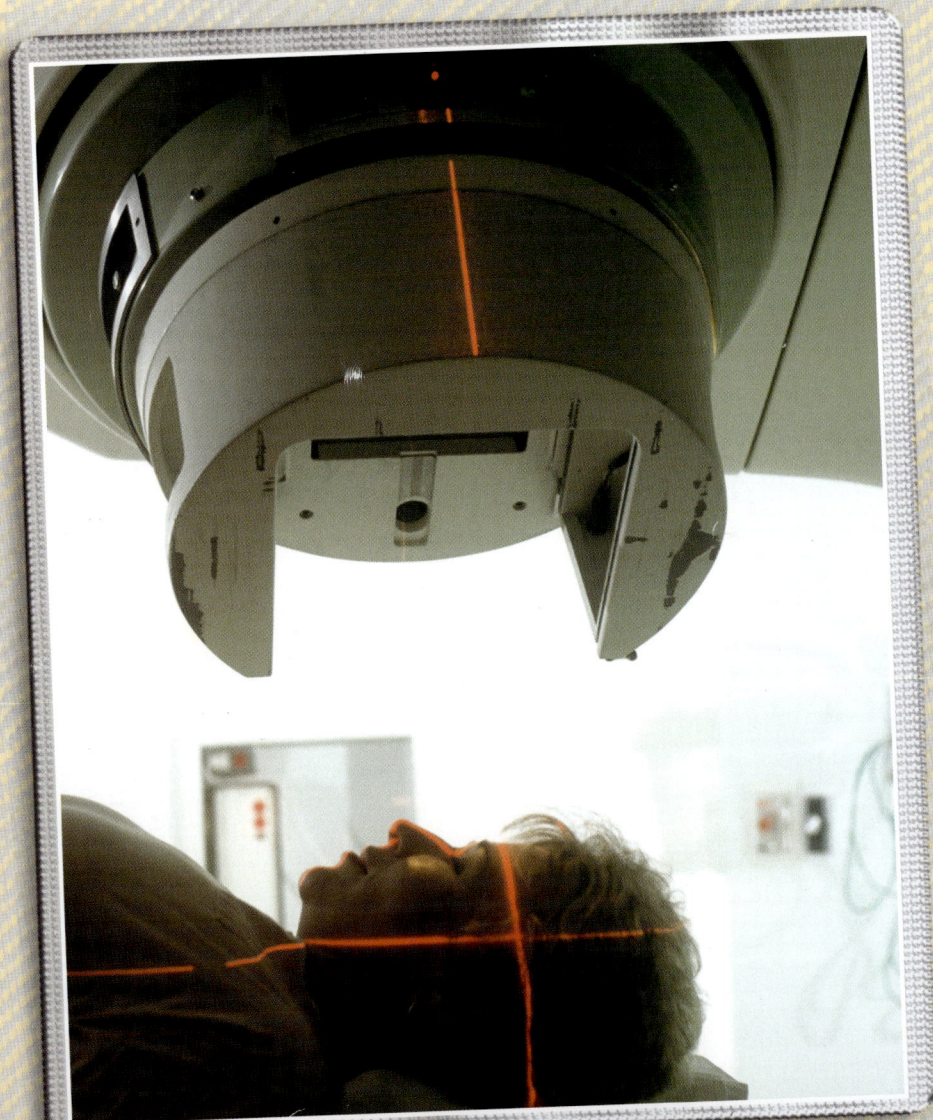

Cancer patients receive radiation therapy. Radioactive ions strike a tumor, killing the cells that make it grow. The radiation can shrink, and even destroy, a tumor.

Dropping the Bomb

Einstein gave us the knowledge we needed to figure out atomic energy. He also unintentionally gave us the power to create weapons of mass destruction.

If you have not heard of atomic bombs, or **nuclear bombs**, it is because many years ago, the world learned a hard lesson about the destruction they can cause. Splitting atoms unleashes tremendous amounts of energy. That is why nuclear power plants must take special precautions to ensure that reactions do not spin out of control, like they did in Chernobyl. So why would anyone want to create a machine whose fission reactions could not be controlled? War.

In 1941 the entire world was at war. Germany, Japan, and Italy were on one side, called the Axis Powers. Great Britain, Russia, and France were on the other side. They were called the Allies. The United States joined the Allies in December of that year after Japan attacked the U.S. naval base in Pearl Harbor, Hawaii. By this time, Japan and Nazi Germany were very powerful.

Nuclear bombs were tested in the deserts of New Mexico before they were used on Japan. After the war, the United States continued testing in Nevada (*pictured*) in search of a more powerful weapon.

The Nuclear Non-Proliferation Treaty was put into effect in 1970. The document is signed by 187 countries. It limits the construction of new nuclear weapons. It also calls for the disarmament, or destruction, of nuclear weapons that already exist and encourages the peaceful use of nuclear energy. Surely, the treaty was influenced by seeing the destruction these weapons could cause.

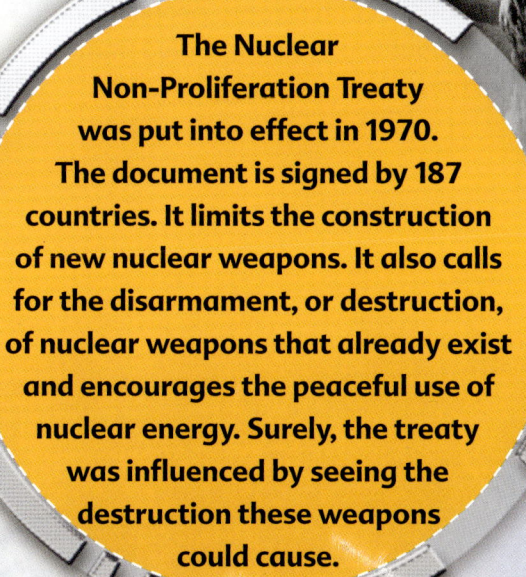

Scientists from around the world gave up their positions to join the top-secret Manhattan Project. Among them was physicist J. Robert Oppenheimer (*far left*).

The United States received dreadful news. The Germans had already figured out how to separate uranium-235 from its isotope, uranium-238. This was the first step in creating plutonium, a highly radioactive element. In 1941 Germany was leading the nuclear arms race. Because of a tip from Einstein, the United States decided to act quickly. The top-secret Manhattan Project was formed in 1942. Scientists from around the world were recruited to create a nuclear weapon.

That same year, the first small controlled explosion took place in Chicago. Manhattan Project scientists had figured out how to separate uranium-235 from uranium-238. They quickly began to work on a solution.

By April 1945, Germany had surrendered. The world knew that the Allies had won the war. Yet, Japan would not surrender. In fact, the Japanese were preparing to continue the war.

Hiroshima, a city in Japan, was destroyed by the atomic bomb "Little Boy" in 1945.

On August 6, 1945, President Harry S. Truman gave the order to drop the first nuclear bomb on Hiroshima. "Little Boy" was made with uranium-235. Every building within a one-mile (1.6 km) radius was destroyed. About 70,000 people died immediately from the blast. Some turned directly into ash. Farther away, the light and heat burned clothing onto people. Over five years, about 200,000 people died from radiation poisoning.

This helmet and tricycle were pulled from the ruins of Hiroshima. Very little survived the bombing.

Three days later the United States dropped another nuclear bomb, made from plutonium-239, on Nagasaki. "Fat Man" was even more powerful than "Little Boy." Luckily, much of the city had been evacuated two days earlier. Yet, the death toll was still horrible. By 1950, 140,000 people were assumed dead because of the bomb and radiation. Japan surrendered just five days after the Nagasaki bombing.

No other country has ever used nuclear weapons. President Truman explained that the bombs ended the war. He sacrificed the lives of thousands for the lives of millions. Yet, there are many people who still believe it was wrong to have dropped such powerful bombs.

Today, Hiroshima and Nagasaki both depend on nuclear power for most of their energy. For decades, testing of nuclear weapons continued in the United States. Bombs were blown up over the Nevada desert, with no understanding of the effects of radiation in the air. In 1963 air testing of nuclear weapons was banned. In 1992 U.S. president George H. W. Bush signed a bill ending underground testing.

There is now a global fear of nuclear weapons. A few countries own more than enough nuclear weapons to destroy the entire world several times over.

In 1995 Boris Yeltsin was the head of Russia. He was told that a nuclear missile was heading toward his country. His military was on high alert. He was about to retaliate with a nuclear weapon of his own. At the last minute, he learned that it was a false alarm. It was not the first close call for an accidental nuclear attack.

Nuclear Fusion

Most of the energy in the universe comes from atomic energy created by nuclear fusion. Scientists have not discovered how to control it or use it yet.

Nuclear fission uses elements with large nuclei. Atoms of elements are split to release energy. In **nuclear fusion**, elements with smaller nuclei are used. In a fusion reaction, two nuclei join together with an explosive release of energy. Fusion releases more energy than fission.

Like many stars, the Sun constantly undergoes fusion reactions. The result? Heat and light.

Just how much energy is produced through fusion? The Sun is an example of a source that is powered by fusion. In fact, all stars are powered by fusion. Clouds of dust and atoms clump together when **gravity** pulls them in. The pressure heats up these balls of matter to millions of degrees. When it is hot enough, fusion occurs. During a fusion reaction in a star, two hydrogen isotopes strike each other. Their nuclei fuse and an atom of helium is formed. The first time a fusion reaction occurs marks the birth of the star. A huge amount of light and heat is released. This energy triggers additional fusion reactions that keep the star alive. The reactions push back against gravity. The star grows as matter is pushed away with each explosion.

Fusion reactions only occur at extremely high temperatures. The atoms must be heated to millions of degrees. We have only begun to understand how to control fusion reactions. We cannot depend on them for energy—yet.

The hydrogen bomb, or H-bomb, is powered by fusion. First, a fission bomb acts like a trigger. It provides the energy needed to compress the hydrogen atoms. This enables the hydrogen atoms to heat up enough to begin fusion reactions. H-bombs were tested in Siberia between 1952 and 1963. They turned out to be about one thousand times more powerful than bombs made through fission alone, such as those dropped on Japan in World War II.

In a fusion reaction, the molecules of two small atoms combine. They become one new atom, releasing neutrons and energy.

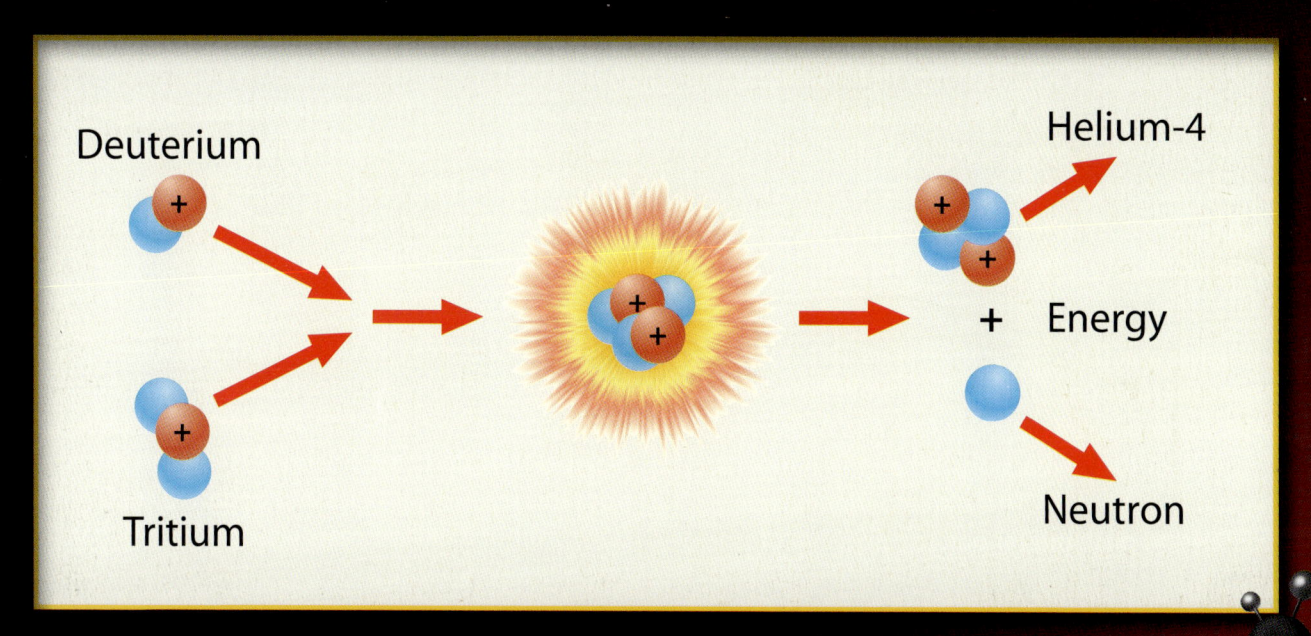

Deuterium + Tritium → Helium-4 + Energy + Neutron

35

When some stars die, they explode in a supernova. Supernova explosions are quite beautiful.

Without the fusion reactions in the Sun, there would be no life on Earth. The energy from sunlight gives life to plants. Plants perform photosynthesis, in which energy from sunlight is used to make food. A waste product of photosynthesis is oxygen. Without the Sun, organisms could not perform photosynthesis. Without photosynthesis, there would not be oxygen on Earth. Life would not survive.

Fusion reactions occur in all stars. This is what makes them bright. Eventually, after billions of years, a star will run out of helium and hydrogen isotopes for fusion reactions. When this happens, the star begins to die. There are no more fusion reactions to push matter out. The pressure of gravity makes the star collapse in on itself. The size of a star determines what happens next. When a very massive star collapses, all the matter that was once expanded is now shrunk into a small space. The pressure is too much. One final explosion called a supernova occurs. It is one of the brightest and most powerful explosions in the universe. It pushes gas and radiation out into the universe.

Our universe would not be here if it weren't for fusion reactions. According to the Big Bang Theory, our universe began as a hot, dense mass of subatomic particles. The universe expanded from this mass of particles and began to cool down. About a million years later, galaxies began

Big Bang

300,000 years after the Big Bang: The dark ages of the universe begin. The universe is filled with energy and matter, in a thick, dark fog.

400 million years: Stars form; mini black holes form from the stars' deaths.

1 billion years: Galaxies begin forming. The dark ages end.

Galaxies evolve

9.2 billion years: Sun, Earth, and solar system have formed

13.7 billion years: Present

to form. Exactly how is still unknown. What we do know is that fusion reactions made their formation possible. Astrophysicists, scientists who study the physics of space, hope that by understanding fusion, they can understand our universe.

What happens after a supernova explosion? Some supernovas become black holes. How exactly do these black holes form? After the explosion, the star's core collapses under its own gravity, forming a black hole. Some of the matter that exploded out is pulled back in. As more matter is pulled in, the gravitational pull becomes stronger. Over time, the black hole becomes so powerful that nothing—not even light—can resist falling into it.

Exploring Space with Atomic Energy

Einstein's theories opened the doors for scientists searching for a way to release the vast potential energy in atomic nuclei. We can use those same theories to understand our universe.

Earth orbits the Sun because the Sun is so massive. Black holes, which form when stars die, are much more massive. Planets, stars, and even solar systems can be pulled in. Yet, no one has ever seen a black hole. Since not even light can escape from it, a black hole cannot be seen. However, we know they exist.

Picture a whirlpool of water in the drain of a bathtub. It swirls. Other things, like soap suds, get pulled down the drain with the water. The same is true of black holes. A star breaks apart as it is pulled into a black hole. It releases gases and energy. All of these pieces eventually disappear into the black hole.

The star on the left was close enough to the black hole to fall in. The arrow shows how it breaks apart and spirals in. The red gases illustrate the energy that is released in the form of X rays.

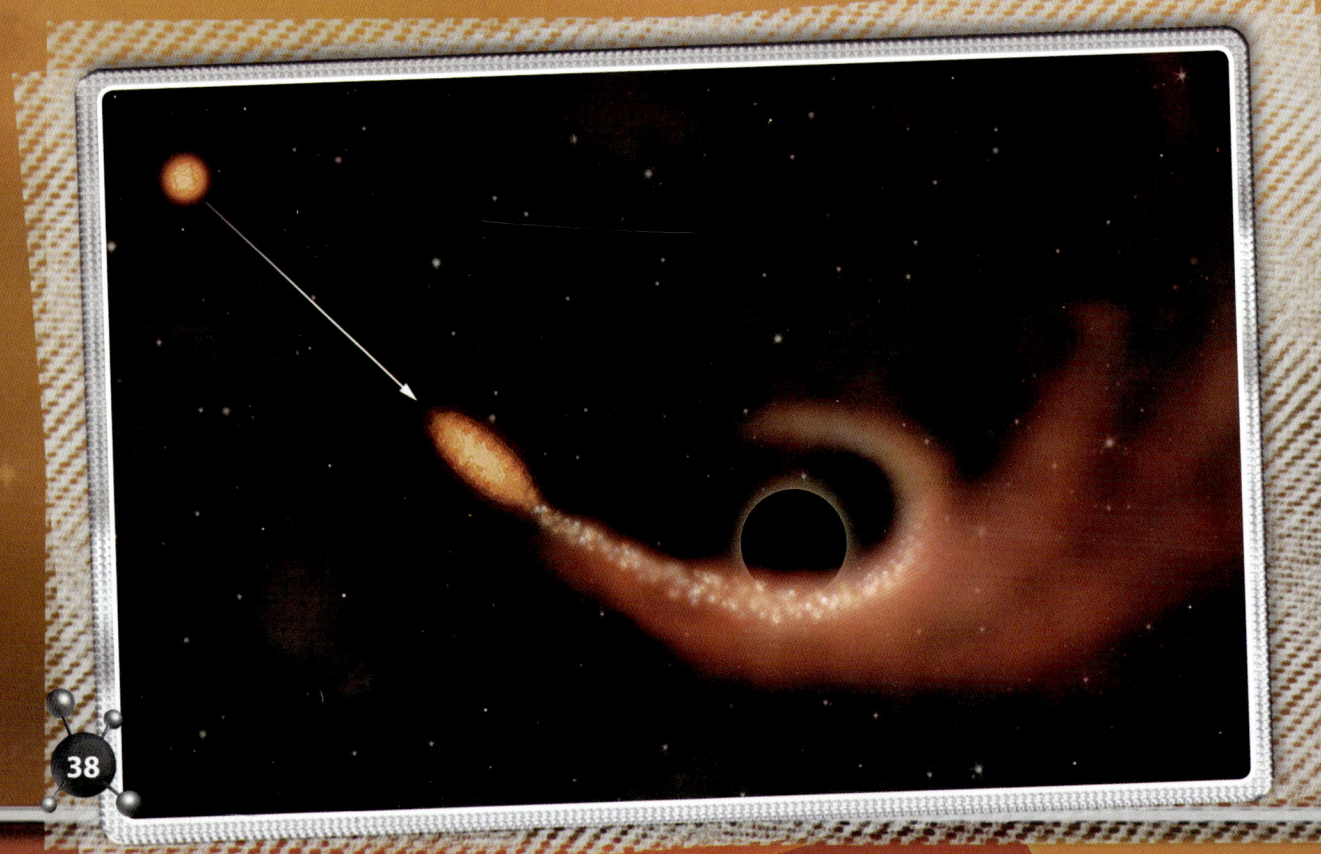

The LHC particle accelerator will help scientists study subatomic particles.

Two of Einstein's theories, the General Theory of Relativity and the Special Theory of Relativity, predicted this behavior. NASA (National Aeronautics and Space Administration) has tools that can detect large quantities of X rays in space, which often means a black hole is present.

Einstein's Special Theory of Relativity describes particles moving near the speed of light, which is 186,000 miles per second (300,000 km per second). Most scientists agree with Einstein's theory, but it has been very difficult to prove on Earth. We look at particles in space for evidence to support his ideas. The X rays around black holes are an example of such evidence.

There is another way to study high-speed particles. We can attempt to recreate the conditions found in space. How? By using the same technology used in radiation therapy. Currently, particle accelerators are being used to speed up subatomic particles for research in astronomy. Scientists study particle behavior at near light speeds.

The largest particle accelerator ever built is called the Large Hadron Collider (LHC). Scientists plan to use it to speed up particles and have them collide. Many people are afraid of what will happen if they do this. What if they create a mini black hole? Can it suck up the Earth? Will the radiation destroy the world?

The chances of the LHC creating a mini black hole are very small. Yet, this is exactly what scientists hope to do! They remind people that cosmic rays produce more radiation than the LHC ever could, and we're still alive. If a mini black hole was created, it would be smaller than an atom. It would exist for fractions of a second before evaporating. Yet, scientists are interested in studying the particles that would be left after it disappears.

Electrons

High-speed electrons

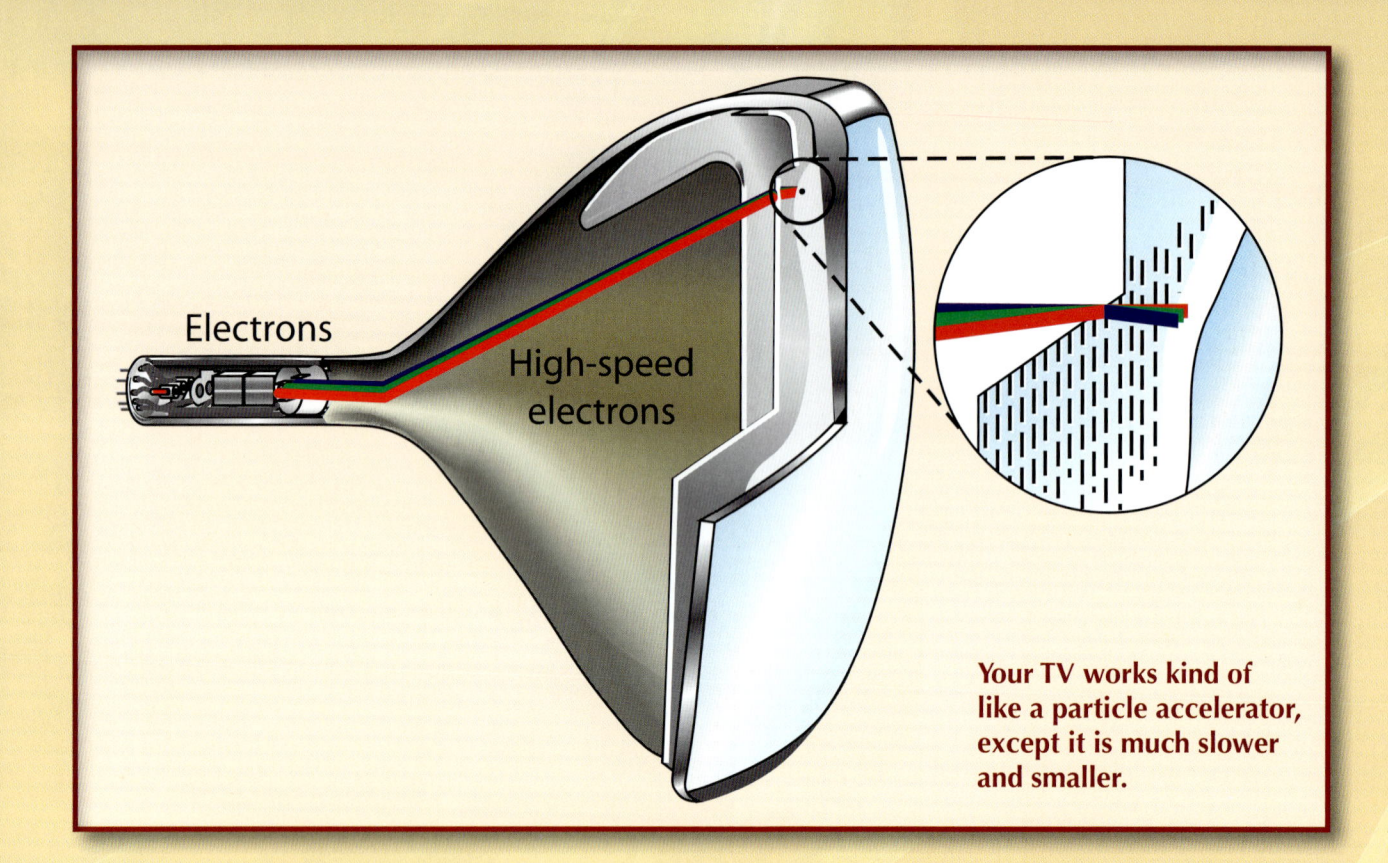

Your TV works kind of like a particle accelerator, except it is much slower and smaller.

The bottom line is that the LHC cannot possibly create a black hole that would put our planet in any danger. In fact, particle accelerators are used every day.

Your TV and computer display screens use particle accelerators. A cathode ray tube speeds electrons up and then changes their direction. The high-speed electrons crash into molecules on the screen. When they do, light radiates. It takes the form of pixels, which are the smallest units of information in a screen image.

Of course, a cathode ray tube is much smaller and much slower than the LHC. Some people are excited about the possibility of a mini black hole. They think it may allow us to travel through time.

If the LHC can create a mini black hole, it might also be able to create a wormhole. A wormhole is a tube that would allow travel between two regions of time and space. At one end of a wormhole is a black hole. At the other end is a white hole, which shoots matter out into space. Many movies have been made about the possibility of time travel through a wormhole. In fact, scientists have even studied this possibility.

However, even if a human could survive being pulled into a black hole, we're a long way from creating a useful one. Any black hole the LHC could make would be so minuscule that an attached wormhole would barely be large enough for an atom to pass through.

40

Of course, people always want to believe. If the possibility of time travel for an atom exists, who is to say that, one day, we humans will not be able to time travel? Perhaps in the future, technology will be developed that will be able to withstand the pressure of a black hole. Or, perhaps we on Earth will receive a visitor from hyperspace—a theoretical region where people can travel faster than light. There are many unanswered questions about space and the future. No one knows what the future holds. One thing is certain though: a door to that future will not be created by the LHC!

Using a particle accelerator to study subatomic particles has been compared to throwing a TV off of the Empire State Building and gathering the pieces. Trying to figure out how a TV works from those pieces would be pretty hard! So is trying to figure out how subatomic particles work by using a particle accelerator.

In theory, time travel through a wormhole is possible.

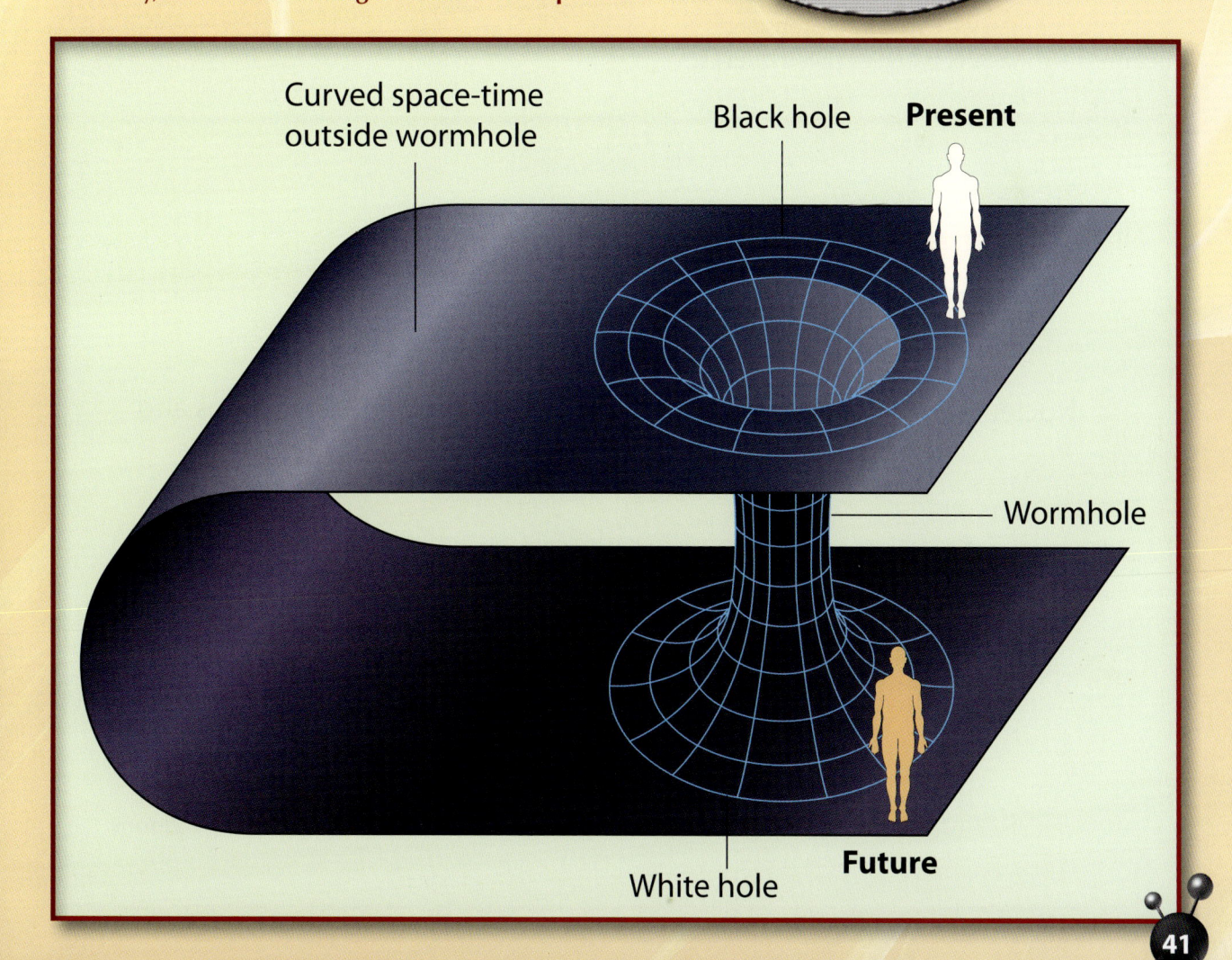

Curved space-time outside wormhole

Black hole

Present

Wormhole

White hole

Future

41

The Subatomic Zoo

Advances in science have shown that there are bits of matter than we can't even imagine. Physicists are studying the particles that make up protons and neutrons.

Until the 1930s, scientists believed the atom could not be split. They were wrong. Scientists soon began wondering if subatomic particles could also be split.

An American physicist named Murray Gell-Mann suspected that subatomic particles were even smaller than we thought. Protons and neutrons are made of particles called **quarks**.

It is believed that even before hydrogen nuclei existed, there were quarks. At the beginning of the universe, these particles were thrown through space. Eventually, they came together to form protons and neutrons. It is also believed that all quarks in existence are as old as the Big Bang. However, they were not discovered until the late 1960s.

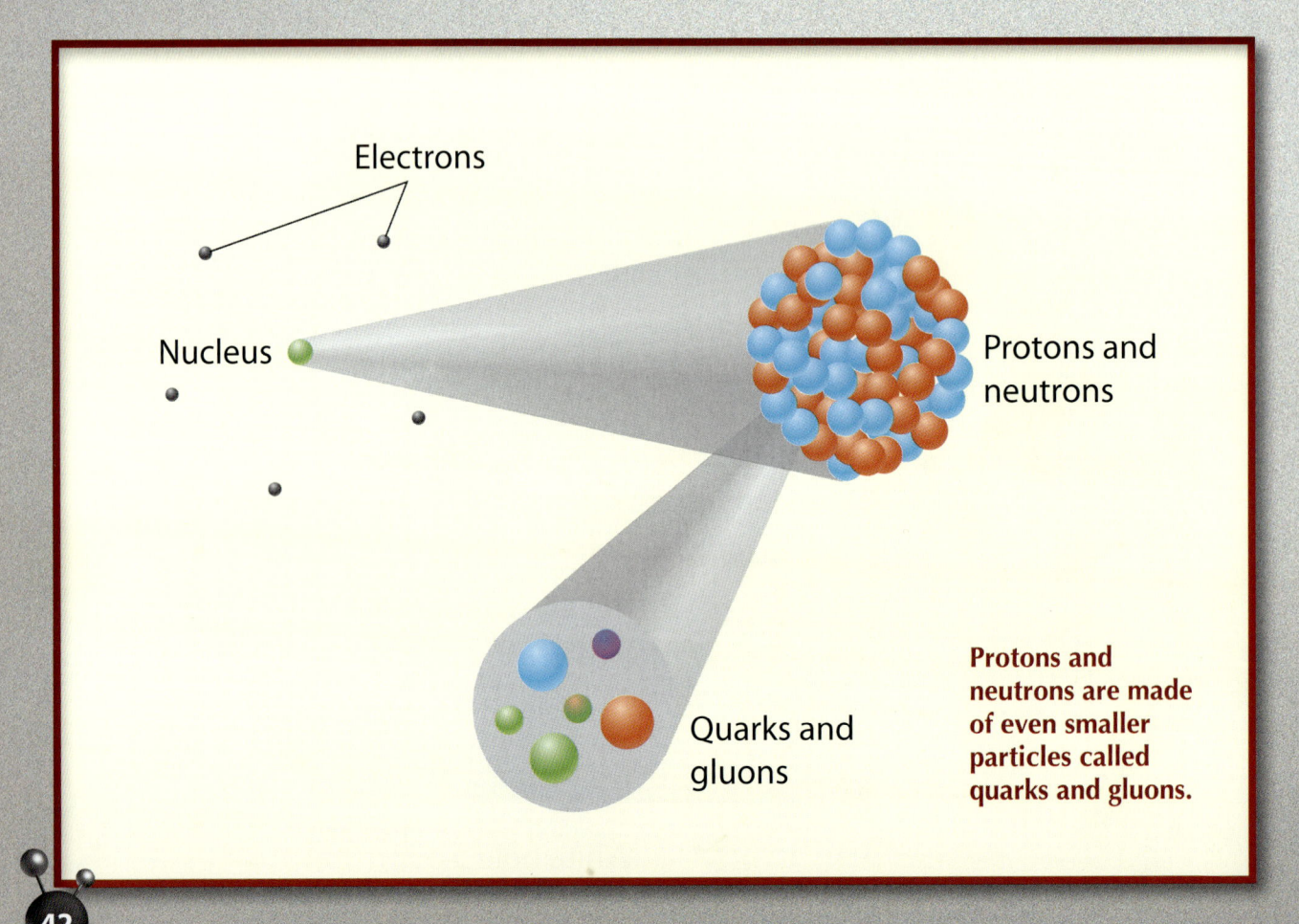

Electrons

Nucleus

Protons and neutrons

Quarks and gluons

Protons and neutrons are made of even smaller particles called quarks and gluons.

Quarks are held together by even tinier particles called **gluons**. They got their name because they act as a glue that holds the quarks together to form protons and neutrons. There are different types of quarks. The combination of these types determines what kind of subatomic particle the quarks will form.

Other than the Gell-Mann theory, there is no proof that quarks exist.

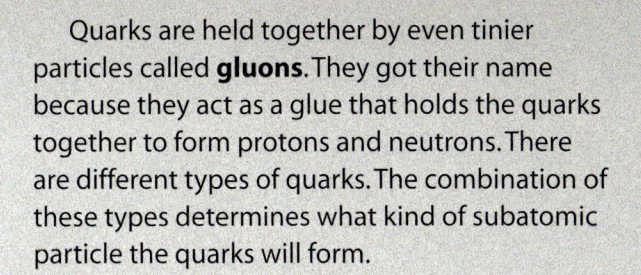

Scientists also wondered how protons and neutrons stayed together inside the nucleus. Protons are not attracted to neutrons. Particles called mesons explain this. A meson is a pair of quarks with opposite charges. The way mesons combine can explain the attraction between protons and neutrons.

There was one final mystery to the atom. Scientists knew electrical forces kept electrons in orbit around the nucleus of an atom. Still, they wondered what caused the forces. They found **photons**, which are particles of light energy. They have no mass because they are all energy. They move at the speed of light. The action of photons can be compared to ping-pong balls. Electrons and protons bat the photons back and forth between each other. This constant batting causes a strong electrical force that connects the electrons to the nucleus.

Murray Gell-Mann knew how to have fun with his work. He discovered that there were different types of quarks, and he even got to name them. He sorted them by positive or negative charge and mass. Each category was a different flavor. Some of the flavors are up, down, strange, charm, and beauty. They also have colors!

Scientists can understand the purpose of some of the subatomic particles discovered, but others are just bizarre. In 1932 astronomers studying cosmic rays, or rays of energy that reach Earth from space, made a startling discovery. They already knew that small amounts of radioactive particles reached Earth, but one of the particles was very strange. It had the same mass as an electron, but it had a positive charge.

Scientists named this new particle a positron. The name is short for positive electron.

They also found that when a positron meets an electron, they both disappear. They destroy one another. Why? Electrons and positrons are antiparticles, which means they have the same mass and the same strength of charge, but their charges are opposite.

Neutrinos have little mass and no charge. They do not react with many other particles. Most neutrino detectors are underground. They are filled with a fluid that reacts with neutrinos. The larger the detector, the more neutrinos it can detect. What amazing fluid is used in this high-tech device? Water!

When stars explode, energy is released. A neutrino detector confirmed that Earth is constantly being struck with subatomic particles from space.

Scientists found that radioactive decay emits energy. Yet, it does not emit as much as they expected. Where does the energy go? It is carried away by subatomic particles called **neutrinos**, which are the most mysterious particles that have been discovered. They have no charge and almost no mass. This makes them very hard to study.

These are just a few of the quarks and subatomic particles that exist within the invisible world around us. Scientists say these particles belong in a subatomic zoo. To cover them all would take another book! Discovering these particles has increased our knowledge. However, scientists are not sure how that knowledge can be applied. It is up to curious minds like yours to find out!

Where do neutrinos come from? For starters, they come from space. Scientists thought that neutrinos were constantly slamming into Earth, but there was no way to be sure. That all changed in 1987 when a supernova explosion was visible from Earth. Days later, neutrino detectors in Japan and Ohio detected nineteen neutrinos. That number may seem small, but considering how hard neutrinos are to detect, nineteen was pretty amazing! It was the first proof that exploding stars could emit neutrinos.

Glossary

atomic number The number of protons in the nucleus of an atom.

DNA Deoxyribonucleic acid; hereditary material that controls the activities of a cell.

electron A negatively charged particle that orbits the nucleus of an atom.

fossil fuel A nonrenewable resource such as coal or oil.

generator A device that turns moving energy into electrical energy.

gluon The subatomic particle that holds quarks together to make protons and neutrons.

gravity A force of attraction between two objects with mass.

ion A charged particle.

mass How much matter an object has.

matter Anything that takes up space, has mass, and is made of atoms.

molecule A substance formed by two or more atoms chemically combined.

neutrino A particle that has no charge, almost no mass, and travels at nearly the speed of light.

neutron A particle in an atom's nucleus with no charge.

nuclear bomb A bomb that unleashes the power inside an atom's nucleus.

nuclear fission The process of splitting an atom's nucleus to release energy.

nuclear fusion The process of joining the nuclei of two atoms to release energy.

particle A very small piece or part of something larger.

photon A particle of light energy and the basic unit of electromagnetic radiation.

positron A subatomic particle that has the mass of an electron and the charge of a proton.

proton A positively charged particle inside an atom's nucleus.

quark The unbreakable particles that protons and neutrons are made of.

radiation Energy released in waves from the nucleus of an atom.

radioactive Undergoes spontaneous emission of energy as the nucleus breaks down.

turbine A device that turns potential energy in water into kinetic (moving) energy.

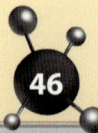

Find Out More

Books

Morgan, Sally. *From Greek Atoms to Quarks*. Chicago: Heinemann, 2008.
Discusses the discovery of the atom, its subatomic particles, and how quantum physicists are using this new knowledge to further our understanding of the world around us.

Oxlade, Chris. *Atoms*. Chicago: Heinemann, 2007.
Includes information about atoms, from their structure to how they are used in nuclear energy. Also includes six experiments that you can perform at home.

Wheeler, Jill C. *Eye on Energy: Nuclear Power*. Edina, MN: Checkerboard Books, 2007.
Discusses the history and future of nuclear energy. Includes helpful illustrations and information about nuclear wastes and weapons, accidents and possibilities.

Websites

http://www.eia.doe.gov/kids/energyfacts/sources/non-renewable/nuclear.html
The U.S. Department of Energy has a website with many informational links related to nuclear energy.

http://www.howstuffworks.com/search.php?terms=split+atom
This website offers multiple articles explaining fission, fusion, atom smashing, nuclear energy, and more.

Index

atomic theory, 6–7, 18

Big Bang Theory, 36
black hole, 37–41
Bohr, Niels, 21

carbon, 10–11
carbon-14 dating, 12, 16
Chernobyl, 25, 30
Curie, Marie, 14, 28

Dalton, John, 6–7
Democritus, 7

$E = mc^2$, 18
Einstein, Albert, 18–19, 30–31, 38–39
electron, 7–10, 12–13, 17, 19, 21, 35, 40, 44
element, 5–7, 9–15, 19–22, 27, 31, 34
Empedocles, 7

Fermi, Enrico, 20–21
fission, 21–24, 30, 34–35
fusion, 34–37

Gell-Mann, Murray, 42–43

Hahn, Otto, 20–21
hydrogen, 9–11, 35–36
hydrogen bomb, 35

ion, 7, 12
isotope, 12–14, 18, 20, 22–23, 25–26, 31, 35–36

Large Hadron Collider (LHC), 39–41

Meitner, Lise, 20–21
Manhattan Project, 19, 31
molecule, 9, 11, 12, 40

neutrino, 45
neutron, 12–14, 18, 20, 22–23, 35–36
nuclear bomb, 30, 32–33
nuclear medicine, 26
nuclear power, 22–25, 30, 33
nucleus, 8, 10–13, 15, 17–22, 26, 35

periodic table of elements, 10–11
photon, 43
plutonium, 23, 31, 33
positron, 26, 44
proton, 8, 10, 12–13, 21, 35, 44

Rutherford, Ernest, 8, 10
radiation, 12–18, 20, 22–25, 31–33, 36, 39

Special Theory of Relativity, 18, 38–39
Strassmann, Fritz, 20–21
subatomic particles, 21, 36, 39, 41, 45
Szilard, Leo, 19

Thales, 7
Thomson, J. J., 7
time travel, 40–41

uranium, 10, 13, 14, 16, 20–25, 31–32

wormhole, 40

X rays, 17, 27–29, 38–39